Mostly Maggie at Doggy Day Camp

by

Barb Norris

Published by
Melange Books, LLC
White Bear Lake, MN 55110
www.melange-books.com

Mostly Maggie at Doggy Day Camp ~ Copyright © 2013 by Barb Norris

ISBN: 978-1-61235-670-9

All rights reserved. This book, or parts thereof, may not be reproduced in any form without permission from the publisher; exceptions are made for brief excerpts used in published reviews.

Stories in this book are based on actual events in the dog day care industry and encompass multiple dog day care facilities. All dog incidents are true. Names have been changed to protect the innocent.

Cover Art by: Becca Barnes

Mostly Maggie at Doggy Day Camp
Barb Norris

Never boring. Usually rambunctious. Rarely quiet. Occasionally stubborn. Sometimes silly. Often noisy. Always unpredictable. Always lovable. Always fun. Meet the dogs of Doggy Day Camp.

Dedicated to
Dog Lovers Everywhere

It was the lowest paying,
most physically demanding job
I've ever had.
It was also the most fun,
most rewarding job
I've ever had.

I was a
Doggy Day Camp Counselor.

I hope you enjoy reading "Maggie"
as much as I enjoyed writing it.

"You want me to put my hands Where?"
"Geez, Sassy, already?"
"Good morning, Maggie, my girl."
"You left the playroom door open."
"Hey, you two, let's break it up down there."
"Ouch!"
"Not on your life, Spider Guy!"
"Oh, yuck, Clyde. Don't slurp that."
"Wags. Wags! WAGS! Pulee-e-e-s-e be quiet."
"Okay, who's responsible for that puddle?"
"No, Maggie, you cannot eat my shirt."
"Time for a belly-rub, Snowball?"
"Excuse me, dogs. Make way for the mop lady."
"Are you telling those dogs a story?"
"Ouch!"
"Pulee-e-e-z-e don't make me go in there."
"Scally. No. Not in the drinking water."
"WHOA!"
"Wags, you'll see Scally in just a minute. Don't carry on so."
"Ah-rooooo-ooooo-rooo."
"What are you selling? Hot dogs?"
"Sorry, Casper, there will be no more flying today."
"Thank you for the kiss, furry face. I love you, too."

Mostly Maggie
at Doggy Day Camp

Table of Contents
The Road to Camp	1
Up Close and Personal	8
Good Morning, Maggie	14
In the Big Playroom	19
Parade Day	28
Daisy In Distress	34
Good Morning, Scally/Wags	37
Who Let the Dogs Out?	40
A Snowball Meltdown	46
Excitement in the Small Room	50
Inside Out	53
Stuff Happens	58
All Dogs Like Me	62
Houdini Dogs Identified	65
A Soggy Doggy Day	70
An Unsound Test	77
Where There's No Smoke…	81
Small Room Happenings	86
Sucker for a Shelter Dog	90
A Scary Situation	94
Another Day – Another Collar	98
More Stuff Happens	102
Outside In	106
Good-bye, Campers	110
Choose Wisely	112

~ The Road to Camp ~

Sixty years old and I needed to find a job. Imagine that. I wasn't crazy about going back to work, but it just didn't make sense not to. I was only two credits shy of qualifying for Social Security benefits in a couple of years. I didn't have to earn a ton of money. I could work part-time, and I wouldn't have to work for very long.

It had been twenty years since I'd held a job. I was a receptionist, then an executive secretary, and finally an office manager. I thought this area would be the logical place to start. I thought wrong. I'd been out of the work force so long that what few computer skills I had were now obsolete. Oh, I could learn whatever programs would be necessary, but employers were not prone to accepting less than immediate skills. I also wasn't the sweet, slim young thing I'd once been. Yes, that was still important to many companies. I could pretty much give up on an office job.

Then there was the little problem of my hearing. It had started to fail while I was still employed. This would make it impossible for me to be a court reporter. My transcripts might be really fun to read. Fun, yes, but accurate? Probably not even close. Besides, if I heard or thought I heard an outrageous statement by a witness, the defendant, a lawyer, or even the judge, I'd be rolling my eyes and muttering under my breath. I'd likely be cited for contempt and end up in jail.

A 911 dispatcher was out of the question as well. I'd be a real danger to whomever needed help. I'd gladly send it, just not always the right kind of help and probably not always to the right place. That would not be good.

There was also the issue of my hands shaking. No one knows why, but I've had shaky hands as far back as I can remember. Combine that with the hearing thing and I wouldn't last ten minutes as a waitress. Getting orders wrong and spilling coffee all over my customers would not get me many tips, no matter how friendly I was. In fact, it probably would get me fired in short order. I guessed I wouldn't make it as a sculptor either. It was immediately and abundantly clear to me that being a brain surgeon was definitely out of the question!

Enough with what I couldn't do. Whatever the case, I still had to find a job. Okay, so I had a few hurdles to overcome. As if it weren't going to be hard enough, my stubbornness kicked in. I was not going to settle for just any old job. Being a chronic and stubborn optimist, I decided I'd go for a job I would really enjoy. Time to get serious about this whole thing and figure out what I could do that I would also like to do.

What I truly wanted was some kind of work with dogs. They wouldn't care that I was technologically challenged. They wouldn't care that I was no longer young and svelte. They wouldn't care if I didn't hear them exactly right and if my hands were not rock-steady. Realistically, though, I did have to admit I had a few limitations in this area as well.

I couldn't possibly foster dogs. After ten minutes in my house, any foster dog would be my dog—forever. Besides, that would be a volunteer position and there wouldn't be a paycheck. A vet's office was out of the question. I'd be too upset about sick or injured animals that couldn't tell me what hurt. I was positive I would not be able to deal with any necessary euthanasia. A shelter or rescue would definitely not be good: I'd want to take every animal home with me. It was also possible that I'd be arrested for assaulting any animal abuser I could identify. Once again, I conjured up visions of spending time in jail, and I knew I wouldn't look good in prison garb. I had no official qualifications to be a dog trainer, so that was not an option either. Actually, I didn't have any qualifications beyond common sense and a great love for animals, dogs in particular.

After searching for several months, I spotted an ad for a pet supply chain building a new store close to home. They strongly urged people to rescue puppies or kittens from shelters, or to go through a reputable breeder. The store didn't sell these. They did, however, sell rabbits, ferrets, guinea pigs, and other small critters, as well as birds, snakes, lizards, amphibians, fish, and a variety of spiders, scorpions, and the like. They were looking specifically for people to care for these animals and try to put them into good homes. I would be good at that as long as I could avoid the spiders, scorpions, and millipedes. I wouldn't be working with dogs, but I would be happy working with almost any creature. This job was actually a possibility.

Off I went to apply. The initial interview went pretty well. When I found out that there were plans to include a Doggy Day Camp in the store, I was absolutely beside myself with joy. Now that would be a job I knew I'd enjoy. In fact, it sounded like the perfect job for me! I couldn't imagine any job that could possibly be better. The store would open within a month, but the Day Camp facility would not open for three to four months. The lady doing the interviewing saw my excitement and was apparently impressed I was willing to wait. Wait I did, periodically checking in with the store. On the one hand, I didn't want to pester them to death. On the other hand, I didn't want them to forget me.

Finally, after almost four and a half months, I got the call I'd been waiting for, and I went in for a second interview. I thought it went well, and I was feeling pretty good about it. A few days later, they called and offered me a counselor position in the day camp program. YES! I was thrilled.

Having landed my perfect job, I was anxious to start. I would be working with a variety of dogs—all shapes and sizes. I was on my way to becoming a Doggy Day Camp Counselor. I didn't know it then, but I was also on my way to meeting Maggie.

My duties, as far as I knew at the time, would be to play with the dogs, keep them busy, and break up the occasional little doggy squabble. Of course, there would no doubt be some of what my friend calls the 'Poop-Scoopin' Boogie' to add a bit of interest. This really would be the absolutely perfect job for me. How hard could it be?

Apparently, it would be a little harder than I'd thought. I was off to training classes.

These classes were not exactly what I had anticipated. I found out that I would just have to wait to meet the dogs. First, I would have to attend one week of customer service training classes required for all new employees, regardless of their position. During that week, I was in class with several other folks, all of whom were much younger than me. They were not all headed for the day camp program, and that was good news for me. After the general training, there would be two weeks of intensive training for working with the dogs. I was anxious to get this show on the road, but I also knew any information I picked up would be worth the time somewhere down the line.

We started with some basic retail public relations. We would smile a lot. If we didn't know the answer to a customer's question, we would find the answer person in the right department. We would smile a lot. We would put price stickers on merchandise. We would smile a lot. We would do a little cashiering. We would smile a lot. We would stock shelves. We would smile a lot. We would collect shopping carts from the parking lot. We would smile a lot. We would police the area outside the store. We would smile a lot. We would not take up any of the closest fifteen parking spaces. Oh, yeah, and we would smile a lot.

I had to learn a little bit about all kinds of critters, mostly of the furry, cuddly variety. I was happy to learn about bunnies, ferrets, rats, mice, and guinea pigs. I picked up some good information about birds and their general health. I learned a little about fish and aquariums. I'm happy to report that I can now efficiently bag up a fish for a safe trip home.

There wasn't much emphasis on snakes and lizards, which I do like and have no trouble handling. There are some good-looking snakes and lizards that tend to slither, but they are not slimy, as some people believe. There was virtually no class in the creepy, crawly critter category. That was okay with me. You have to be a special kind of person to handle scorpions and tarantulas. Animal lover that I am, I am definitely not the kind of person to handle any creature with more than two wings or more than four legs. Just the thought of touching these creatures makes me shudder.

At last, it was time to start training for the dogs. Our teacher was a professional animal behaviorist/trainer. I mean a no fooling around big-time trainer. Her name was Elena, and she was a delightful lady. I liked and respected her from the beginning. Her resume was impressive and her background was awesome. She had worked in Hollywood, not only with dogs but also with lions and tigers and bears. Oh, my!

Early on, I found out what the real duties of the counselors were. There was a bit more to the job than I'd expected. I would not be a dog trainer, but I would have to exercise some alpha authority over the dogs. My official job title would be Doggy Day Camp Counselor. While this title sounded far more impressive than dog-sitter/janitor, I really didn't care what they called me. I'd be right where I wanted to be.

First and foremost, I'd spend most of my time in the playrooms with the dogs. My primary duty would be to let the dogs play with each other without human intervention. Sometimes, though, to keep the dogs happy and active, I would have to toss a ball or instigate another activity of some kind. Wow! I couldn't imagine getting paid for having that much fun.

I would also have to get down and dirty. There would be dishes to wash, windows to wash, floors to vacuum, wash, and sanitize, toys to get out and later pick up, sanitize, and put away. Geez, it was a lot like home, now that I think about it. There would be furry faces to wipe down when the dogs drooled excessively. Globs of this drool would have to be wiped off the drooler, other dogs, the equipment, the walls, the windows, the floor, and the counselors. There would be water dishes to be filled, refilled when the dogs drank a lot, refilled after the dogs spilled them, refilled after the dogs played in them, and refilled when a dog would occasionally decide to add water of his own to the drinking dish. Last, but certainly not least, there would be a lot more of the ever-popular Poop-Scoopin' Boogie than I would have ever thought possible.

The camp had no outside facility for the dogs to use for normal bodily functions. What we did have was an elimination station, a room that contained a toilet to flush solid waste, a hose to wash the room down, and two fake fire hydrants. Well, I had a few questions.

Would the dogs actually use this room as intended? Would they really use the fake fire hydrants? Would house-trained dogs spend the day at camp gritting their teeth or would they do their business inside the camp? Would they then go home and totally forget that they'd ever been house-trained in the first place? Would this bring an onslaught of disgusted and angry pet parents to our doors?

I was told these very questions had actually been researched. It had been found the dogs would not to mess up their crates while they were at camp and would still follow house rules at home, because they are not fond of soiling their own territories. We were also told that the dogs would indeed do their business in camp whenever and wherever nature called. The camp playrooms were mutually shared territory and not exclusive so they did not feel compelled to keep the place clean. In the playrooms, the dogs had no inhibitions. NONE. At all.

Employees brought in their own dogs during training so we could practice our newly gained knowledge and skills. There was an adult Great Pyrenees, very calm and cooperative. There were a couple of small dogs, a Dachshund and a medium sized mix of unknown ancestry. They were a patient lot as they were put through the evaluation procedure. We played with these dogs and practiced our authoritative alpha voices to maintain order in the playrooms and in the kennel area.

There were basic rules of doggy etiquette that I had to know. I learned what subtle signs to look for in order to anticipate and, hopefully, avoid possible doggy squabbles. How the dogs held their ears and heads would be clues. I did already know that a wagging tail isn't always a sign of a happy dog. I found out there was a lot more to it. Sometimes a wagging tail was a subtle sign of distress and sometimes of aggression. How they were wagging combined with other visible factors told us a bit about them. I soaked up as much information as I possibly could.

Evaluating a dog for entry into the camp program was of prime importance. Not all of the dogs were suitable for camp, and these dogs were not invited back. One employee had three dogs that she wanted in the program. Two passed muster. One didn't. We enjoyed all the dogs, but we didn't play favorites with who would be accepted into camp. We couldn't play favorites. Allowing a misfit into camp could lead to disaster.

This particular camp didn't automatically exclude any specific breed. The so-called bully breeds—Pit Bulls, Rottweilers, or Dobermans, etc.—were evaluated just the same as any other breed. Each dog earned his way into the program on his individual merits, not by breed reputation. If all tests were passed, the dog was admitted to camp.

Individual evaluations were the best way to meet a prospective camper. It was important to get to know a dog quickly, and to try and establish a bit of a bond. This was my favorite part.

During the first two weeks of the camp's public opening, counselors were being evaluated right along with the dogs. We also had to be suitable candidates for camp life. Elena was on hand to watch evaluations, our interaction with the dogs, and with their people. It was kind of a nervous time for counselors. If enthusiasm counted at all, though, I was in pretty good shape.

Puppy-sitting with dogs who already had good homes. Wow! How great would that be?

~ Up Close and Personal ~

The first step in evaluating any applicant was talking to the prospective camper's people. No problem there. I can discuss dogs 'til the cows come home. I needed to find out as much as possible about the dog's likes, dislikes, allergies, etc. For example, it was a very good thing to know that Fido or Fidette absolutely hated to be hugged. If I actually remembered this little tidbit of information, it would keep me from hugging that dog and keep him from chomping me.

It was most important to pay attention to any of Fido's food allergies. Poisoning one of my furry charges with a well-intentioned-but-lethal treat would be devastating. I couldn't even imagine having to tell someone I'd accidentally poisoned his or her adored dog. Oh, my gosh. I'd carry guilt with me for the rest of my natural life. Besides, I could possibly end up being sued. They sure wouldn't get much, but I still didn't want to be sued for the wrongful death of any animal or any person. I paid very close attention. I checked health records to be sure the dogs were current on shots and that they had been spayed or neutered.

Having collected all the information I could, it was time to meet a client dog, one on one, using everything I had learned in class. Of course, our class dogs had been right with their people all through training. I wondered what would happen with a dog I'd never met before.

The real fun began when I, a virtual stranger, took a dog away from his beloved mom and dad and into a quiet room. Most of the dogs looked at this as an exciting adventure. This was already a good sign. Some of the dogs became a little nervous when they realized that mom and dad were not right behind them. Almost all of these slightly apprehensive dogs calmed down very quickly once they realized I wasn't an evil, wicked dog-hater with murder or dognapping in my heart. A very few of the dogs were shaking and quaking, they were so nervous. These really scared ones were not generally good candidates. Camp would be no fun at all for a truly terrified dog. We would suggest a socialization class for skittish dogs. Once they passed such a class, they would be re-evaluated for camp entry.

Then it was time to get up close and personal. I mean seriously up close and personal!

First, I gave the dog a very quick health check. There were a few very basic areas that could be easily checked even without veterinary training. This was general information that I figured could be useful with my own dog. I learned as much as I could learn.

I ran my hands all over the dog's furry body, looking for any skin problems, open lesions or vermin. Yep, my hands went everywhere just like the judges in dog shows, only more so. Most of the time, the dog tolerated it well. Talking to him the entire time drew attention away from my hands and to my voice. Boy, if I was good at talking about dogs, then I would have to say I was great at talking to them. I've always talked to dogs. Then I checked the ears, looking for any obvious problems there. I made sure his eyes were clear and bright. So far so good.

Most dogs don't particularly like to have their feet touched. We did have to check them in spite of the general dislike. This was not a problem for me, because I'd checked my own dog's feet daily when he was a puppy running around a new back yard that was all clay with no grass. I found if I started by petting his leg and gently worked my way down, the dog would not jump and pull his foot back. That was the method I used for camp hopefuls. It worked well.

"You want me to put my hands where?" I already knew the answer to my question. I had asked as a delaying tactic while I worked up my courage. These were not the dogs we'd had at training with their people right there and this might get tricky, too tricky. It was time to check the condition of the dog's teeth and gums. I had to be able to see inside his mouth, top to bottom, front to back. Sometimes this could be tricky since it was kind of hard to get them to smile on command. Most of the dogs cooperated, but there were a few who were a little reluctant to flash those pearly whites. In those cases, it required lifting the dog's lips up and sometimes exerting gentle pressure to pry his teeth apart without putting your fingers between his uppers and his lowers. That could end up being painful.

I finished the physical examination, and I thought it had gone pretty well. I ended up with the same number of fingers that I had before I started the exam. I was never bitten during exams.

Temperament tests were next. I gave the dog some food or treats in a dish. Then I stirred the food around and pulled the dish away from him while he was eating. For this, I was using a pole. It wasn't a good idea to move things around or approach the dish with my hand. It was too risky. If the dog was aggressive, I'd find out the instant he bit me. A food-aggressive dog would not be admitted to camp.

Once the food test was passed, I gave the dog a toy. This was a two-fold test. I wanted to know if he was overly possessive with his toys. There is a big difference in a dog wanting to play tug or keep-away with a toy and one who doesn't want to share at all. Here again, I used the pole to move the toy away from him. Once I knew the dog wasn't going to rip me to pieces, I played with him for a short time. How he played showed me more of his personality and would demonstrate, at least to some degree, his activity level.

Based on what I learned from the evaluation, I made a somewhat educated determination on which of two playrooms the dog would find more comfortable. The large playroom had windows looking into the camp lobby and into the store itself, presenting a lot of visual distraction. The dog could see what was happening outside the playroom. This was the right room for confident, friendly, and active dogs.

The smaller room had no access to public activity. This was the room for dogs who had a hard time coping with too many distractions, dogs who were just a little too nervous to interact with extremely active dogs, or older dogs with low activity levels. On the rare occasion this room was in use, it was generally for small dogs. There were, of course, exceptions. My own older sixty-pound dog, Toby, on the only two days he attended camp, was much happier in the smaller, quieter room. There was a Briard, a fair sized dog, who also preferred the smaller room. For a counselor who wanted a fairly calm day, this was the room of choice.

A dog's size had very little to do with room placement. We had a Chihuahua who loved to run with a Great Dane. We also had a Yorkie that loved the excitement of the big room. It always amazed me that these little ones didn't get trampled by the big guys. Dogs apparently have no concept of size. To them, a dog is a dog is a dog.

Having successfully passed these steps in the evaluation, it was time for the final exam. This was the Big One. Meeting the other campers. It really wasn't a good idea to just throw a new dog into an established group and hope for the best. That, we'd been told, would be inviting trouble. As an added safety precaution, whichever counselors were working anywhere in the store at the time all came to the playroom for the introduction of any new camper.

A portable rod fence was put into place just inside the big playroom, separating the newcomer and the evaluating counselor from the group. One of the familiar dogs, proven to be mellow in any situation, was also put into the enclosure. The other counselors were stationed outside and right next to the fence, just in case any dog became overly upset, too excited, or suddenly aggressive. The new dog went one on one with the calm dog inside the enclosure and then nose to nose through the fence with the dogs gathered on the other side.

If all went well, both the calm veteran and the new dog on the block were released into the playroom to run around with the rest of the gang. All available counselors were alert for any signs of trouble. On more than one occasion, a dog had passed all the preliminary tests, but became very aggressive when meeting the entire group with no fence separating them. When that happened, the aggressive dog was immediately removed from the room and was rejected for camp. A socialization class was suggested and the dog would be invited to try again after passing such a class.

It took only a few minutes of mutual sniffing, slurping, and butt-wiggling for everybody to be best friends. Or for the counselors to find out that maybe their room placement decision should be reversed. Once introductions were made and all the dogs were getting along well, it was time for extra counselors to leave the room and go back to other duties while the dogs all got down to some serious play time.

The evaluating counselor then went back to talk to the dog's people. This was normally a good experience for the dog's family and for me. On rare occasions, we did have to turn down a dog for camp. This was never easy, but it was something that had to be done.

Counselors had a standard set of equipment for working in the playrooms. The most important was your voice. When a dog wasn't behaving, the first thing we tried to do was distract him by making an unusual noise. This most often got his attention and he went back to acceptable behavior. If this didn't work, we had a couple of options.

There was a spray bottle of plain tap water to discourage excessive barking or other unacceptable behavior. We had a slip lead with us at all times, in case we had to stop and contain or remove a dog. We also had a spray can of Citronella.

This was to be used only for extreme situations. I didn't know exactly what the Citronella did to them, but I was told the dogs definitely did not like it. I didn't ever want to find out first-hand what it did. I suspect it must have burned their eyes something fierce. In my mind, a situation would have to verge on absolute, undeniable catastrophe for me to use it. I didn't want to see a catastrophic situation, and I didn't want ever to have to do anything that would hurt the dogs, even if it were temporary.

I can't forget sanitation. We all danced the Poop-Scoopin' Boogie a lot. Mop buckets filled with sanitizing cleaner and water were used far more often than any of us would have liked. These buckets were really important, and they absolutely had to be changed often. Sanitizing liquid dispensers mounted on the walls in all areas of camp were available for counselors as well. We all took sanitation seriously. It was healthier for the dogs and the counselors.

There was almost always a receptionist in the camp lobby, who could step in and help with the dogs in an emergency. Camp counselors also worked on the store floor so they weren't always within ear shot. Every counselor in the playrooms had a walkie-talkie to summon help if needed. Any counselor working outside the camp area also had one. These came in handy on more than one occasion. The primary function of the walkie-talkies, however, turned out to be to call in a replacement when it was time for a break from the playroom. Very important.

Mostly Maggie at Doggy Day Camp

The probation period had ended. I had passed everything. My review had gone well. Elena had moved on to training folks at other locations. Now it was officially official. I was a full-fledged doggy day camp counselor - the Senior Counselor, no less. I didn't ask whether the Senior part of the title was given to me based on merit or whether it was because I was, by a long way, the oldest employee in the entire store. Either way, I was a real happy camper myself.

Meet new dogs with respect, a smile in your voice, and a touch of caution.

~ Good Morning, Maggie ~

I was in charge of opening the camp. It was seven o'clock in the morning and I'd made my rounds. The playrooms were clean. Toys were clean and in the playrooms. Water dishes were filled and in place. Climbing toys were set in place. Doors were all secured. Other counselors would be in by the time playtime began at eight o'clock. I was ready for the day.

The camp was located at the back of the store and opened at seven. The store itself didn't open until nine o'clock, so a portable check-in desk was set up just inside the front doors during those two hours. Check-in was pretty routine. The receptionist greeted each dog and his people, and took note of any special instructions for the day. This paperwork would follow the dog throughout the day, notes being made for the pet parent if necessary. The dog was given a very quick physical once-over. His own collar was replaced with a special break-away camp ID collar, a safety rule for the dogs. Should another dog happen to get hold of this collar it would immediately come apart, preventing choking or other injury.

Once the receptionist finished checking in a dog, she paged a counselor to come and take the dog back to the camp's kennel area and put him into a crate. There he waited, often vocally and never patiently, for playtime to start. The dogs were always anxious to socialize and were happy and feisty on arrival.

"Barb, Maggie is here," my walkie-talkie squawked at me from the front check-in desk.

As I headed up front, I couldn't help but smile, remembering the first time I'd seen Maggie. She was a gorgeous fawn-colored Great Dane. Her front paws were up on the desk, and she towered over her mom, our receptionist, and me. The ear-cropping had not exactly taken on her. Her ears sort of stood up, but the tips did not. They fell over just a little. To me, that just added to her obvious charm. Maggie and I had bonded instantly. It was love at first sight.

I was excited to meet her. Maggie was excited to meet everybody. She was drooling all over the desk, drooling all over the floor, drooling all over her mom, drooling all over the receptionist, and drooling all over me when I reached over to pet her. I took Maggie with her unusual ears back to the kennel area and directed her into a crate. She was a happy, friendly, and absolutely magnificent dog. I couldn't wait to see her in the playroom with the other dogs. Before that could happen, though, I had to get back out to the desk and get my initiation into drool-cleaning. Oh, boy. That had been about four weeks earlier. Maggie and I had become great friends since that first meeting.

When she spotted me coming, Maggie began wagging her tail furiously. She was a great one to start my day because she was always so exuberant. Her first order of business was to jump up on me. I expected this, but it still threw me slightly off balance and I crashed into a sign that stood behind me.

"Good morning, Maggie. How's my girl today? Okay, okay, you can get down now."

I did manage to keep my feet under me long enough for Maggie to get off of me before any damage was done. It was very hard to be stern with her when she was so obviously happy to see me. She was completely lovable, and I have to say that I absolutely adored her.

Maggie was our most regular camper, coming in at least three, and then four days a week. She was also our biggest camper. She was only eight months old and still had that puppy-clumsy thing going, which made things mighty interesting when that puppy weighed in at one hundred twenty pounds and was still growing.

Maggie was familiar with the normal routine—walk, calmly, we hoped, back to the kennel area and into one of the large crates until playtime began. The process was normally routine and uneventful. Normally but not always.

Barb Norris

This particular day was not a normal day. The large crates were not available because of maintenance work. No way was Maggie going to fit into one of the smaller crates. What the heck would I do with her while I was on my own and other dogs were coming? I came up with a plan.

"Well, Maggie, it looks like you get to skip the crate and get right into the playroom." Maggie was happy about that. Because it was still early and we were the only ones back there, I could stay with her. There were lots of windows so I could keep an eye on the lobby as well. I knew the doors were locked and secure and the windows were all dog-proof. If I absolutely had to leave the room for a minute or two to collect another camp arrival, there was nothing in that room that could cause her any injury. I felt comfortable this would work until another counselor arrived. For the time being, though, it was just Maggie and me.

First thing she did when we entered the room was to look around for her buddies. None of them were there yet. I could see the "Hey, where is everybody?" look on her face. It only took her a second to get over her disappointment though. After all, I was right there and Maggie was more than happy to play with anybody. It didn't matter to her whether it was another dog or two, or a counselor.

Since I was obviously the playmate of the moment, Maggie jumped up on me again, knocking my magnetic ID badge off my shirt. The badge was a little bigger than a business card, and Maggie decided it was a wonderful chewy toy. Her very favorite game was Keep Away, and the Leave it! command was completely lost on her.

"C'mon, Maggie, you can't have that. Bring it here."

This was not what Maggie wanted to do. It was time for another plan.

I decided a little charade might be the best plan of action. The trick was to get close enough to her to get hold of anything at all that she'd had. To do this, I pretty much had to pretend to ignore her and nonchalantly just happen to stroll rather close to her. Then, without looking like I was looking, I needed to make a quick grab and get my hand on whatever it was I wanted to take away from her. Once I'd gotten hold of it, Maggie would almost always let go without much of a struggle. Using this strategy, I managed to retrieve my badge in reasonably short order.

Mostly Maggie at Doggy Day Camp

I was about to put my badge back on when Maggie spotted a small something on the floor. Maybe a yummy snack? I jammed my badge into my pocket and headed over to retrieve the whatever-it-was. Well, it must not have tasted so good because she dropped it immediately. It was a small stone. I had no clue as to just where that had come from. No wonder she'd spit it out. I picked it up quick as all get-out and headed for the kitchen to dispose of the stone, happy she hadn't chomped down on it. A broken Maggie tooth would definitely be a problem. I gave Maggie a glance along the way. Uh-oh.

"Now what have you got, Maggie?"

She'd found something else to chew on. It was small, black, flat, and rectangular. It took me a minute to realize it was the magnet backing from my badge that had been on the inside of my shirt. Obviously, it had fallen out. Now magnets cannot possibly be good for a dog to eat. The stone was stuffed into my pocket along with my badge, and I went after the magnet. She did not want to give it up.

Maggie thought this was a really fun game, and I had a hard time keeping up with her keep-away self. I had just done my nonchalant act, and she wasn't buying into that again so soon. She finally dropped the magnet, quite accidentally, I'm sure, and it landed partly under one of the supports on the climbing bridge. I threw caution to the wind and did a hard belly-flop down onto the bridge, wedging the magnet underneath where she couldn't get hold of it. I was finally able to retrieve it. Whew. Now was my chance to leave the playroom. Oops.

I spoke too soon. Maggie had other ideas. After all that excitement, she had to relieve herself, big time, which meant a major clean-up job. That chore being done, I successfully left the playroom and went into the kitchen, pulling the bottom of the Dutch door closed behind me, once again giving Maggie a glance. Oh, no.

Maggie was standing about twelve feet back from the Dutch door doing a whole lot of I-bet-I- can- make- it-over-that-short-little-door foot-shuffling and backside-wiggling. If I didn't stop her, she would sail over the door into the narrow kitchen area, not nearly big enough for a safe landing. If she made it over that door there was no doubt it would result in severe injury to Maggie, to me, and to the kitchen. Not a pleasant thought. This required an immediate plan.

Distraction. Distraction. I had to be quick about it. I called her name, clapped my hands, and jumped up and down long enough to get her attention. It worked. She stopped her jump preparations. I got a grip on the top half of the door and closed it. Whew, now I could breathe a little easier.

A second counselor came in about that time. Thankfully, on this day, no new arrivals showed up before that second counselor.

Sharon was surprised to see Maggie in the playroom already. It wasn't play time just yet. I told her that the big crates were not available.

"Maggie is loaded for bear this morning," I told Sharon. "She's more than a little feisty today. Just so you know."

"Well, I can take this room today if you'd rather not." Sharon offered.

That she mentioned this surprised me since we all shared any unusual behavior about any of the dogs. I told her I didn't have a problem working with the rowdy dogs in the big room. I guess she thought, because I'd mentioned it, that I didn't want to work with Maggie. It was nice of her to offer, but that really surprised me. No way was I angry with Maggie. In fact, I never got upset or angry with any of the dogs.

It had been an exciting day so far, and the real day hadn't even begun.

A happy dog, even giving you a little happy flack, is a great way to start a day.

~ In the Big Playroom ~

I would estimate the big playroom to be approximately fifty feet long by thirty-five feet wide. It was big. This was where the more active dogs played. It had four doors, the Dutch door into the kitchen the most often used. There was a door into the elimination station from the playroom as well as an opposing door from that room into the kitchen. There was a double Dutch door separating the big playroom from the small playroom. There were also double glass break-away doors from the playroom into the store itself.

This room also contained a portable bridge made up of two sections, with steps on one end and a ramp on the other. When put together, the sections, each about five feet long, formed a center platform about two feet high. The dogs loved it. They'd run up and down the length of the bridge. They would race up to the top and sit on the bridge. They sat on the steps of the bridge. They would zoom in and out under the bridge. They jumped over the bridge. They ran around the bridge. They curled up on the steps of the bridge. They hid under the bridge. Sometimes, the counselor would run up and down the bridge, and occasionally the counselor would sit on the bridge. It was definitely a well-used, multi-tasking bridge.

Maggie, first one in as usual, bounded into the playroom fully expecting to see friends there. She slammed on the brakes and her face clearly said, "Hey. Where is everybody?" First dog in almost always made that same face.

Since I was the only other living being in the room, Maggie assumed I was her playmate of the day. What this meant, as far as she was concerned, was that jumping was just the ticket for instant entertainment. She, of course, assigned herself the role of the jumper and I, of course, was the designated jumpee.

Now I appreciate a good dog hug as much as the next guy, but with her front paws on my shoulders, Maggie stood at least fifteen inches taller than I did. Jumping up on people, uninvited, was something we discouraged regardless of the dog's size. I convinced her to get back down to her own four feet. She did. Then, she got ready to try it again. I strongly discouraged her, and she was okay with that.

She was okay with that only because Snowball had just come into the playroom. Maggie knew that, unlike me, Snowball would run around the room like crazy with her. She was sure right about that. Counselors did not run in chase games with any of the dogs. Even if you had a head start, the dog doing the chasing would catch up. If it was a small dog, little paws could be a little painful when they hit the backs of your legs. If it was one of the big dogs who caught up with you and jumped on your back, your face would be introduced to the floor fast. No, you definitely did not want to chase around with the dogs.

Snowball was a Great Pyrenees, a big white dog who was as stable and mellow as a dog can be. She was a young adult, very calm, and was like a den mother to everybody else. Whenever Snowball was in camp, almost always since she came in with her person, another counselor, she was the first dog introduced to new camp candidates. She ran with the big dogs, played gently with the little dogs, and was a real sweetheart. When Snowball took a rest, which was often, she usually allowed the smaller dogs to climb on top of her, curl up next to her, and get in her face. On the rare occasion when she was not in the mood to be bothered, she quietly let them know, and they left her alone.

Snowball loped over to Maggie. They put their noses together in a quick hello and started racing each other around the room. Maggie jumped over the bridge, Snowball ran around it, and the two were very busy with each other. Both Maggie and Snowball gave Bonnie and Clyde a quick glance when they entered the room, ignored them, were ignored right back, and continued to race.

Bonnie, a Maltese, red hair bow always in place, and Clyde, a small cream colored Malti-poo, were housemates and hung out together at camp. The two of them zipped up to the top of the bridge and wrestled with each other. I went over to the bridge, leaned down to tell them hello, my attention first on Clyde. He was a pretty good cuddler and absolutely loved people attention. Next thing I knew, Bonnie had her front paws on my head, raking them through my hair. She was obviously a graduate of hair dressing school because she was combing my hair. She didn't like the way it looked that day? I turned my attention to her. Both she and Clyde were wagging and slurping each other and me like crazy.

Bonnie was the more sociable of the two and would sometimes play with the other dogs for a few minutes, if Clyde would allow it. He was extremely jealous of her, though, and would bark furiously at whatever dog had the temerity to approach her. As small as he was, Clyde at times could evidently be intimidating to the other campers, no matter their size. Either that or the other dogs found his barking so annoying they would back off just to get him to be quiet. Whatever the reason, it almost always worked. The offending dog would head off to other activities.

Another dog entered. It was Sassy, a mix of questionable ancestry who was on the small end of being medium sized. Sassy liked both Snowball and Maggie and briefly joined in the on-going race. Bonnie left the bridge to give Sassy a friendly greeting, which sent Clyde into a jealous fit, and he started barking. This bothered Sassy not at all. She had too much to do to spend time arguing with Clyde.

However, with the appearance of Benny, a miniature poodle, Bonnie was instantly abandoned. She returned to Clyde on the bridge. He was extremely happy to have her back, lavishing her with slurps and tail-wagging, which Bonnie eagerly accepted and returned.

Sassy dearly loved to play with Benny, definitely her very best camp friend. She dashed over to him, starting a game of Nip & Hide. The rules Sassy had set for this, her own game, were chase another dog, give it a quick nip and run off at top speed. If the other dog was familiar with the game, and even if he had never played before, he would chase her. Sassy loved to get this game going with any of the dogs, big or small. The dogs were not hurt, and this was a fine and dandy game for them.

Not so fine and dandy for the counselor, though. The bad part of Nip & Hide was that Sassy, having nipped another dog, would zoom over and hide behind the legs of the closest counselor, poking her nose out front between the person's knees. This time it happened to be my knees that had now become a shield of sorts. When the chaser came up to the front of me to get at Sassy, my knees were in dire jeopardy. Knee-nipping wasn't really painful, but it tended to be on the uncomfortable side.

"Hey, you two, let's break it up down there,"

In came Duchess, a Lhasa Apso, older and wiser than most of the other dogs. She reminded me of a dowager queen, stately and aloof. I was walking over to give her a good morning pet when I was pushed from behind at knee level. It was Sassy again. It was bad enough when I was standing still, but when I was in motion, especially if I was in a hurry, it placed my entire body at risk. If I happened to fall right on Sassy, it wouldn't do her much good, either.

This little habit had to be broken. I sternly told Sassy to get away. Well I tried to be stern. Anyway, she reluctantly moved off, looking incredibly dejected. I would just be on extra alert and stiffen my knees up whenever she headed my way. Sassy tried it once more, but I was prepared this time. I stiffened my knees and told her NO at the same time. Hopefully, if I did this every single time, she would eventually stop tangling me up. She never did stop altogether. I just got smarter. This time, I made it, unmolested, the rest of the way to greet Duchess.

Once Duchess got her hello pet from me, she chose to ignore everybody and everything, and get right to the self-assigned task of watching the bottom of the Dutch door that led into the kitchen. By golly, if anything or anyone tried to slither in under that door, Duchess would be the first to know. She did occasionally play with the rubber squeaky shoe, but not often. Duchess was getting up in years, and she seemed to think the antics of the whippersnappers at camp were a ridiculous nuisance. She didn't complain, though, and pretty much ignored them.

Cedric, the Dachshund who lived with Duchess, came in with her. Cedric spent most of his day wandering around the room, or sitting on top of the bridge for the duration. He was constantly on the look-out for his mom, Kate, our pet services manager. If he caught a glimpse of her, it was his singular goal to join her. To do this, he tried his best to scoot out any door that opened. He might have been a little older than most of the dogs but he was quick. We all knew we had to be prepared for him to attempt an escape. Cedric, like Duchess, simply couldn't be bothered with the youngsters in the playroom. He never complained either. He was a real gentleman. Everybody loved Cedric, and he got plenty of counselor attention.

"Okay, who's responsible for that puddle?"

I headed over to the handy-dandy mop bucket. When I turned around, mop in hand, it seems the puddle had now become two puddles. Nope, make that three puddles. Once one dog created a puddle, the others couldn't be left out. Even if the dogs gave us a little warning, and we made it to the elimination station, the dogs rarely cooperated. Once in a great while, we'd be successful. Those dogs that used the special room were praised like crazy and petted on their furry little heads a whole lot. They'd get a round of applause from any counselors in the area. Positive reinforcement, but overall, the elimination station didn't fool the dogs for a single minute.

It had gotten fairly warm in the playroom, so it was time to take off my sweatshirt. I got one sleeve off and was working on the other one when I felt a tug on my shirt.

"No, Maggie, you cannot eat my shirt."

I got the sweatshirt off and hung it on the outside handle of the Dutch door, where the dogs couldn't get at it. Silly me. Maggie had been watching me, and as soon as I turned away from the door, she turned toward it. Then, quick as you please, she reached over the door and grabbed my sweatshirt. Fortunately, I was still close enough that I could get hold of both her and my sweatshirt. I convinced Maggie to release it, and I ended up just tossing it across the kitchen, hoping it would land on a shelf and not on the floor in the path of any new canine arrivals. That was the only way to keep it out of Maggie's reach.

Everything was going along just fine. Duchess was at her post guarding the bottom of the Dutch door. Cedric was wandering. Bonnie and Clyde were entertaining each other. Benny, always a fashion plate, went to visit the grooming salon and probably getting his toenails painted blue. Sassy was busy chewing on a rope tug toy. Snowball had spotted someone outside the window and was busy barking her best and biggest bark. Maggie, not to be outdone, dashed over to the window and was now barking her best and biggest bark.

Looming over everyone in the area, front paws on the window, and barking like crazy, Maggie looked and sounded incredibly ferocious. This made most people on the other side of the glass back up a bit. Once she had accomplished her goal of scaring the daylights out of those folks, she lost interest and left the window to return to her camp buddies. After all that barking, Snowball needed a rest. She plodded over to her favorite corner.

"Time for a belly-rub, Snowball?"

She rolled right over. After a few minutes of belly-rub, she rolled back over, put her head down on her paws, and closed her eyes. Snowball took a lot of rests during the day.

"Okay, who did that?"

This time it required both the mop and the scooper. Not the most enjoyable part of this job, but I was becoming an expert in the clean-up department. Everyone needs at least one area of expertise, right?

All the commotion began to die down after an hour or so. The dogs were getting tired and it was time to give them and me a break. I sat on the bridge with both Bonnie and Clyde in my lap. Cedric was as close to me as he could get, and Duchess had made herself comfy under the bridge. Maggie came over and leaned into my knees, looking for a drink. For some reason or other, she preferred to get a drink from me rather than from the water dish.

She was looking for the spray bottle of water. She viewed the water bottle as her own personal sport drink cup. She gently wrapped her mouth around the nozzle and swallowed the water I sprayed down her throat. When she was doing this, she loved the water bottle. However, Maggie also knew that the water bottle was used as a deterrent for bad behavior. When she got a reprimand spray, she hated it. If ever left unattended and within reach, a water bottle became fair game. Maggie would grab it and completely demolish it. For the time being, however, having peacefully slaked her thirst, Maggie stretched out on the floor in front of me.

Snowball sprawled close to the bridge, allowing Sassy to get comfortable right on top of her. Benny, back from the groomer with his nails sure enough painted blue, cuddled at Snowball's side. Everyone seemed to be ready for some quiet relaxation.

Kate was walking through the kitchen. She got just a few steps beyond the Dutch door and then backed up. She knew I was the only one in the playroom and had heard me talking.

"Are you telling those dogs a story?" she asked, not believing that I would actually be doing such a goofy thing.

When I told her that was exactly what I was doing, she just laughed.

Now I don't know if you've ever tried to tell stories to a bunch of dogs, but it seemed like a good idea at the time. So, with a variety of dogs sprawled here and there and everywhere, I told them a story. The story subject didn't matter. It didn't matter to me that they didn't understand a word I was saying. It didn't matter to them that they didn't understand a word I was saying. It didn't matter that anyone hearing me must have thought I was completely out of my mind, telling a story to a bunch of dogs.

I would mention each dog by name every now and then, just to keep all of them interested. When a dog heard his own name in the course of my rambling, he would perk up his ears and cock his head at me. I would acknowledge him, talk to him directly for a minute, and then go on with the story, nonsensical as it was. What mattered was that the dogs were still getting attention, quality time, as it were. I actually got to sit down for a few minutes. That was nice.

"Hey, Kate. Is there any sound connected to the video cam?" I hollered toward the kitchen.

It hadn't occurred to me until Kate asked what I was doing that there might be sound connected to the web-cam mounted on the wall. Clients could check on the playroom action through this on-line camera. While I said it didn't bother me to have people know I tell stories to dogs, it just seemed wiser not to broadcast this activity over the web. Folks would think I really was crazy. Kate assured me there was no sound. I continued my story, comfortable knowing our customers wouldn't think I was completely off my rocker. Ten minutes later we were all back to doggy bedlam, that is, until we began to hear kitchen noises.

Kitchen noises intrigued the dogs. It meant it was almost noon, which meant lunch. Counselors were busy filling food dishes and making sure there was fresh water in every crate. One or two of the dogs put front paws up on the half door and leaned as far into the kitchen as possible. Those who weren't up on the door sat down, listening to the noises in the kitchen, smelling the smells of lunch, and staring intently at the door. They were infatuated. They all liked lunch time.

Of course, kitchen noises also meant it was time to go back into crates for a nap. Luckily, the dogs were thinking only food, not crate time. We started rounding up dogs. Most of these particular dogs were pretty good about going into their crates, and we didn't expect any trouble. I took Maggie back to her crate and headed back for another dog.

One of the other counselors came into the kennel area to report that there were three dogs in the kitchen, not in the playroom where they should have been.

"Barb, you left the playroom door open."

I was stunned. I was a stickler for checking door security, and I was sure I'd closed it. I made a mental note to be extra careful about that in the future. It wasn't a problem this time because the dogs that were loose in the kitchen were Sassy, Cedric, and Benny, all of whom responded to our commands to come and then went cheerfully into their designated crates.

Noon until two o'clock was lunch/nap time. While the dogs were busy scarfing down lunch, it was fairly quiet in the kennel. Once they'd finished eating, however, not all of them were ready take a little snooze. Eventually though, they did settle down and get some rest in spite of themselves.

While the dogs were resting, the counselors were busy sweeping the playrooms, changing the mop buckets, washing the water dishes, often washing the windows, and catching up on any paperwork. Then it was lunch time for us. We rarely raised the same kind of ruckus as the dogs did, though. Yes, we scarfed down our lunches, but we never barked.

Following nap time, fresh water and clean toys were returned to the playrooms. The dogs came back and returned to running, chasing, playing, barking, and such for the afternoon. By six o'clock, most of the campers had been claimed. Tuckered dogs were more than ready to head home and relax with their families.

Then, the counselors got busy with the heavy-duty janitorial tasks.

Playrooms were vacuumed, mopped and sanitized, climbing toys were washed down and sanitized, and crates were scrubbed and sanitized. Toys and dishes were sanitized, and the kitchen floor was mopped. Tuckered counselors were more than ready to head home and relax with their families.

Dogs might not be my life, but I sure can't picture life without 'em.

~ Parade Day ~

Maggie was first to arrive again. The counselors had all been working hard with her to stop her habit of jumping on people. On this particular morning, though, she decided to try it again. She stood up on her hind legs, but then thought better of jumping on me when I held my hand up in a stop signal. She still wanted to jump, but instead of jumping on me, she just jumped straight up using her only hind paws. It looked really funny. I jumped up. She jumped up. I jumped up again. She jumped up again. We did this several times before one of us wore out, that being me, of course. Maggie would have done it again and again and again. Well, she would have done it as long as there were no other dogs in the playroom.

Bonnie and Clyde arrived, and Maggie tried to play with them. They couldn't be bothered. They went into a corner and just wrestled around with each other. In a short while, Duchess and Cedric came. Maggie approached them, but was ignored again. Duchess did her under-door-watching thing and Cedric planted himself on top of the bridge. Usual stuff.

Maggie was feeling somewhat slighted so I jumped with her a few more times until Sassy came. Sassy completely ignored the four quiet dogs and headed immediately over to Maggie, who was finally relieved to have someone here who would run rampant and play with her. The two of them played Tuggie and Chase and were having a grand time.

Pepper, a Black Lab mix, joined the campers. She had very warm, very dark eyes that would melt the Arctic. Her family had rescued her from an abusive situation, and they loved her dearly. Even after all the hard times she'd been through, Pepper was full of love and trust. She loved the dogs, she loved her family, and she loved the counselors. We all hoped we were making a positive impression on her. We thought we were.

Pepper was always happy to be in camp. She zipped over to where Sassy and Maggie were playing Tuggie and joined in the game. Those three played together until they started to run out of steam and decided to take it easy for a bit.

"Oh, yuck. NO Get away from there, you guys." Time for the first mop-up of the day. I was getting really good at this.

Ernie, a delightful Golden Retriever, showed up next. He didn't come in very often and was a welcome sight when he did show up. He was friendly, got along with everyone and was a lot of fun to have around. He was one happy dog. He enthusiastically greeted every counselor as well as the rest of the campers. He and Pepper started a game of Race Around the Bridge and were running to their hearts' content.

We were all surprised to see Duke, a Boxer, when he strolled into the room. He was another one who didn't come often. He didn't have much to do with the little dogs, but he sure did enjoy zooming around with the big ones, and zoom with them he did.

The dogs had been so active that they were all beginning to wear down just a bit, an unusual thing so early in the day. Nobody was running at the moment.

Rambo sauntered in. He was a Rottweiler, the strong, silent type. He paid little attention to the other dogs and even less attention to the counselors. He chose to keep pretty much to himself. He liked to stretch out at the bottom of the front glass doors and quietly try to dig his way out. He would stop trying to excavate the floor as soon as he was told to stop, but the second your back was turned, he'd start again. Tell him to stop, he stopped. Turn your back, he started. This was his regular routine.

He liked to be petted once in a while, but definitely did not like to be hugged, according to the information given by his people when he was admitted to camp. He did play with the other dogs once in a blue moon.

Mostly Rambo liked to be left alone. On this day, though, even he had moved over to join the group and was relaxing with the rest of the gang. Socializing with the other dogs while they were just lounging around seemed to please him this time. He looked content.

I decided it must be time for a parade. I had done this before. Clyde was the best at parade. It was about the only activity Clyde would participate in without Bonnie at his side. Clyde put his whole heart and soul into the parade. He would follow me around the room as long as I was leading a parade. Bonnie would only stick with me about twice around. She actually took advantage of the time on her own to say a proper hello to the rest of the campers. Without Clyde smothering her, Bonnie managed to greet each one of the other dogs. Ernie sort of joined the parade. Mostly he made a lot of side trips to sniff something or just to bounce around the room a little. Rambo half-heartedly tagged along on the tail end for only one round, not really into it. Pepper went only part way around with us, until she realized that her pal, Maggie, was in the parade, too, and then she stuck with us for the duration. Duchess lagged behind but did manage a couple of rounds before going under the bridge for some relaxation.

Cedric never did get in on a parade. He just watched from his grandstand seat on the bridge. He was actually watching for his beloved Kate more than he was watching our parade. He was, I believe, the only dog there who realized what this parade was—just walking and walking around and around for no reason, with no destination in mind and without even any people cheering from the sidelines. He probably didn't think that made sense. Smart dog.

This was great. I was marching along, arms bent at the elbow, swinging in time, the dogs following along for the time being. As I swung my left arm toward the back, my elbow was suddenly enveloped by—what? Oh, a dog mouth. No pressure, not a bite, but my elbow was inside Maggie's jaws. Oooh, this was not good.

Although she certainly wasn't hurting my elbow in any way, I immediately decided that any part of my body that was totally surrounded by a mouth full of canine teeth, no matter whose teeth they were, was not a good thing. The parade came to an abrupt halt, and I got the dogs interested in other things. This was Maggie's first parade. This was Maggie's last parade. No more parades on Maggie days.

Mostly Maggie at Doggy Day Camp

Pepper came up onto the bridge where I was sitting conversing with Cedric and petting Maggie. I turned to greet Pepper, and she surprised me with a slurp on my nose.

"Thank you for the kiss, furry face. I love you, too." I loved all these dogs. They made the job seem not at all like work. A job just didn't get any better than this.

Kate came into the playroom to say hello to the dogs and, of course, Maggie went over to greet her. Maggie had gotten pretty good about not jumping on people unless they invited her. Her retention for more than a week was a bit of a problem, but she really did try. In her excitement at Kate's arrival, though, she jumped up on Kate's back. The problem this time was more than just the jumping. Maggie had her mouth around Kate's one shoulder. She wasn't biting, just mouthing, like she had with my elbow. Maggie had a mouth full of very large teeth that definitely could not be tolerated from her or any of the dogs, no matter their size. Kate and I both sternly corrected her for this new behavior. Maggie had never been so firmly spoken to by either Kate or me, and it must have come as a surprise. She really was a gentle and lovable dog, and she was smart enough to realize that her two biggest fans were not happy with her. She learned immediately that wrapping teeth around anybody's body parts was totally unacceptable. That was the last time Maggie put her teeth around anyone. Thank goodness.

Leaving Kate with the dogs, I headed out for my morning break. When I got back to the camp area, Kate was still in the room with the dogs and she was talking.

"Are you telling them a story?"

"Um-m-m-m. Well, yes, yes I am," Kate replied, rather sheepishly.

"Uh-huh," I said, laughing. "So, I'm not the only one here who does goofy stuff."

The two of us got the dogs up and moving again and things were back to the normal level of running and rowdiness for another hour or so. Then, kitchen noises started.

With the arrival of lunch time, the dogs took up their vigil by the kitchen door. Time to lead them out of the big playroom and crate them. Most of the dogs cooperated fully and it didn't take long to have most of them crated.

Duke surprised us. Last time he was in camp, he did not want to go into his crate. He got right in front of it and would go no further. It took two counselors, one pulling and one pushing to get him in. This time, he was a lot more cooperative. He did not stop outside the crate door. He stepped up and in, slowly and reluctantly, but with no fuss. Well, that was easy.

Ernie, the Golden, never gave us a problem with the crate. He would look like a furry angel, cooperate fully, and hop right in his crate. It was after lunch that he hit his mischievous stride. We didn't know it, but Ernie was an expert at chewing things up. That information had not been given to us ahead of time. It only took one time in the crate, though, for counselors to realize his bad habit.

The paperwork that followed each dog through the day was placed in a plastic envelope and clipped to the door of his crate. It was a good system. When it was time to get Ernie out of his crate for the afternoon, the problem was instantly spotted. Once the counselors had left the kennel area, Ernie kept himself rather busy. He had managed to get hold of the plastic envelope holding his paperwork. He had pulled it through the bars on the door and thoroughly shredded it, along with his paperwork. Fortunately, he hadn't eaten any of the plastic. We found all the pieces. He did manage to swallow a few bits of the paper, though. He would be the dog that really did eat the homework. Ernie cheerfully jumped right into his crate every time. From that day forward, though, his paperwork was clipped to the crate next door.

Then there was Rambo. I escorted him back to the kennel area and he spotted the crates. Rambo just planted his gentle, but strong self as soon as he saw where we were headed. He was nowhere close to the crates. There was absolutely no way Rambo was going into a crate of his own volition. I begged, I coaxed, I tugged, I cajoled, but I definitely did not hug. I was proud of myself for remembering what his people had told me about Rambo not liking to be hugged.

Another counselor took hold of his slip lead and gently pulled him in the direction of his crate. She made it as far as Rambo's neck would stretch and not an inch beyond that point. So I placed myself at the hindmost part of Rambo and pushed. Useless. Rambo did not budge. I lifted his hind end and Rambo was transformed into a wheelbarrow of sorts, his front paws forced to move forward. This was done ever so slowly and carefully. If Rambo didn't move those front paws, he would fall on his chin. We didn't want that to happen, and he sure as heck didn't want that to happen. Slow as it was, he finally went inside. Hooray. Once inside, he calmed right down and didn't kick up a fuss at all. It was just the getting there that created a problem.

The company of furry friends simply has to make you smile.

~ Daisy in Distress ~

Not all dogs are suitable for a day camp setting. One of the hardest things I had to do as a counselor was to tell a family their favorite furry friend would not be accepted. This was a rare situation, and I only had to do it once. Thank goodness.

A day before my probation period ended, I was working with Elena, our teacher. A little mix of unknown origin was brought in for evaluation. Her name was Daisy, and she was exceedingly shy. With a great deal of coaxing I managed to get her away from her mom and take her into the testing area. She barely looked at anybody and was incredibly nervous. Not a good sign.

She cooperated with me during the physical examination, but shook and quaked the entire time. She would not eat from the dish, but she did finally take a treat from me. She would not play with me at all. Her mom was sure she would enjoy camp once she started. I didn't have that much confidence. She barely squeaked through the temperament tests.

The time came to put her into the enclosure. Fortunately, Snowball was at camp. If any of the dogs could put Daisy somewhat at ease, it was Snowball. I led Daisy in. She was petrified. She wanted nothing at all to do with Snowball and was pretty much glued to the door back into the kitchen. That clinched it. There was no way I was going to recommend that this little dog be put into a position that so frightened her. I took her back to the test area.

I was on the floor close to Daisy, but not right next to her. As slowly as I could, I reached out a hand to her, talking softly the whole time. She finally allowed me to stroke her head. Elena had been with us the whole time and asked my opinion. I'd told her I thought Daisy was not a good candidate. She was just too nervous. I felt she was one of those dogs who would spend the entire day cowering in a corner.

Elena agreed. She then volunteered to go out and talk to Daisy's mom. I knew I would most likely have to face this situation some time in the future so I opted to do it myself while Elena was still with us. She would step in if I needed her. She would let me know afterwards if I'd handled it okay, and, if necessary, give me helpful suggestions.

Leading Daisy, we headed back out to the lobby to explain the situation to an anxious pet parent. Daisy's mom was sitting on the floor, and Daisy couldn't get to her fast enough. She planted herself in mom's lap and huddled as close to her as she could. You could see the relief in that little dog's face. I broke the news that Daisy wouldn't be admitted to camp. Daisy's mom was crushed. I suggested socialization classes and that they try Daisy again once she'd passed such a class. Her mom felt awful and tried to convince me I should give her a chance right then. I explained I couldn't do that. She reluctantly left, feeling about as bad as I did. The only one there who was happy to be leaving was Daisy. As soon as they headed out the camp doors she perked right up. She couldn't wait to leave.

Even though Elena told me I'd handled it well, I still felt awful about it. I couldn't get poor Daisy off my mind so I called her mom about a month later, just to see how Daisy was doing, and if she'd been enrolled in a class. I was told she'd been sick, but there were plans to take her to a class. The lady said she'd be back after that class.

Three weeks went by and I had a 10:00 start time at camp. Several dogs were in the big playroom and, much to my surprise, Daisy was among them. She was cowering in a corner of the room. I wouldn't have expected anything else. I asked the other counselor how Daisy had ended up in camp. Nobody seemed to know who, if anyone, had re-evaluated her and approved her. She was scheduled to be there that day until noon. I was anxious to talk to her mom when she came to pick Daisy up, but I never saw her.

Daisy was back the next morning, again cowering in that same corner. I did talk to her mom that day when she came in after the morning session. It was just past noon, and she was expecting to see

Daisy happily running around the room, cavorting with the other dogs.

    The dogs were already crated for lunch. Before I had a chance to ask about classes, her mom got upset that Daisy was not in the room. I told her we had taken all the dogs back to the kennel area at noon, as we always did. She wasn't too happy about that but she did ask how Daisy had gotten along. I told her the truth. Daisy was terrified of the other dogs and terrified of the counselors. Daisy was terrified of everything.

    I never did find out how or why Daisy had been approved. Based on her shaking and quaking, I didn't see how she could possibly have managed in a socialization class. Daisy should not have been admitted.

    That was the last time Daisy was at camp. That poor little dog would have died of fright if she'd had be there on a regular basis. I was glad she wasn't brought to camp again. Daisy wasn't the only dog ever turned down for camp, but she was the only one I had turned down. I was glad I never had to do that again.

    Better to turn a dog down than to see one so completely traumatized.

~ Good Morning, Scally/Wags ~

As I said, normally check-in time was pretty routine. There was one other morning, however, that I won't soon forget. This time it did not involve Maggie. It was customary to replace personal collars with special camp collars at check-in. There were, of course, exceptions, two of them, to be exact.

Their names were Scally and Wags, house-mates. I could see them coming. They were tugging and yanking their dad along behind them as they crossed the parking lot. Now, this fellow was a big, muscular guy, but even he was having one heck of a time keeping up with his two happy and energetic dogs. These two were about as rambunctious as could be. They were sweet, though not so gentle, and they were always geared up into overdrive. It was a whole lot easier to change their collars once they were crated. So, we by-passed the check-in station and headed back to the kennel area. Scally and Wags pulled and tugged while I bounced along behind them, keeping up as best I could.

Scally was a Husky, a mighty handsome fellow. Wags was a good looking, mid-sized Basenji mix, who definitely had not inherited the barkless characteristic of his Basenji ancestry. Wags, in fact, was far and away the most vocal dog we ever had in camp. Scally and Wags were good buddies and did not like to be separated for any reason. We made our way back to the kennels without mishap. These were the only two dogs that were crated together at the request of their people. They both hopped right in without a fuss.

Scrunching down on the floor and bracing myself against the outside of the crate door, I left just enough opening to get my hand inside to remove their collars. I had done this before with no problems. I got hold of Scally and managed to remove his gear. Suddenly, for whatever dog reason, Scally decided to stop cooperating. He was downright determined to get right back out of that crate. I, of course, was just as determined that he not get right back out of that crate. There was a great deal of pushing and pulling going on between us, but I definitely had the upper hand. Then, Wags decided to help his buddy and throw his weight into the fray. Wags wasn't a very big dog and didn't carry all that much weight, but it was enough.

Somehow or other, the two of them managed to knock the crate door clean off its hinges. I'm talking a heavy, bone-breaking, three foot by six foot barred, metal door here. Boy, was I surprised! Thankfully, it dropped right straight down without falling over on any of us or crushing my toes. We had all miraculously managed to escape maiming or death. My knee and the crate frame were now holding the door upright. I couldn't let go of it or it was sure to fall on someone. All I could do for the time being was just not move.

Scally pushed his way past my shoulder, knocking me to a rather awkward sitting position on the floor. I managed to hang on to the door and keep it from falling over. Then Wags took a flying leap over my head and the two of them were running hither and thither. Yon wasn't available or they would have been running there, too.

They couldn't get beyond the main kennel door so they were somewhat contained. In the meantime, Bonnie and Clyde, who had come in earlier, were enjoying the show. Bonnie was sitting at the front of her crate barking now and then. Clyde was zooming around in circles in his crate and was barking like mad. I think the two of them were actually cheering out loud for the two escapees and laughing at me. I'm sure I looked pretty darned silly.

I changed my hold on the door and hung on to it while I pulled myself upright. I found a safe place to lean it and worked on catching up with Scally and Wags. I tried to quiet the two spectators, but they were going to continue to cheer as long as Scally and Wags were running free. All four dogs were having a good ol' time. I was frantically trying to regain control, but was laughing too hard.

Having finished with the door and given up on shushing the two cheerleaders, I came up with an idea. I decided to put the two rowdy ones into the smaller playroom directly adjacent to the kennel area. This took no effort at all.

All I did was open the door to the playroom and invite them to join me. They zoomed right in. They were expecting to see some of their camp buddies. It was too early, though, and nobody was in the playroom yet. That didn't bother them because they still had each other. Since it was almost time for co-workers to come in, it didn't seem wise to attempt crating them again until back-up arrived. Best to leave them in the secure room for the time being.

When Kate and Chris came in, they noticed the absence of that crate door. I explained what had happened, and they started laughing and told me they wished they had been there for the show. The two of them managed to get the door back on its hinges, still laughing at me.

I was laughing at me. It finally hit me that I should have just gone inside the crate with the dogs. It would have been a little cozy but it would have been better than trying to work through the open door. With a little help from Kate and Chris we got the two of them back into a crate. I followed them inside and had no trouble exchanging those collars.

This dynamic duo was one happy handful. They were both in exceptionally fine fettle that day. I could hardly wait for regular playtime to begin.

It is quite impossible to be calm and assertive when you're laughing.

~ Who Let the Dogs Out? ~

Another day had dawned, and I was ready for the action. A quiet day ahead? It was a possibility. We only had four dogs scheduled. Of course, that didn't really mean anything. It wasn't unusual for unscheduled dogs to show up.

In came Snowball. She was the only dog who didn't get the "Hey, where is everybody?" look on her face when she was the first dog in. She glanced around, saw an empty room, shrugged her big white shoulders, got her good morning ear-scratch, and stretched out in her favorite spot to wait patiently for her camp buddies. She didn't have to wait long.

In came Sassy. She dashed over to Snowball and climbed right up on top of her to get her moving. Snowball cooperated and got to her feet. Sassy had rounded up a ball, with which she tantalized Snowball and the two were off and running. That only lasted until there was a pit stop.

"Geez, Sassy, already? Okay, I'll get the mop."

Here came George. He was a Sharpei who was a bit of a touch-me-not. He would tolerate a little petting, but really didn't like any fuss made over him. George, aka Rammer, had a plan that would get him into the Just Try to Take My Ball game. His plan was quite simple. He ran up close to whichever dog had the ball at the moment, Sassy this time. He turned slightly away from her, threw a stocky but impressive shoulder slightly forward, sidled back toward her, and suddenly rammed her. Sometimes this dislodged the ball from the dog in possession. Sometimes it didn't. It didn't seem to matter who actually had possession of the ball, they all just kept at it.

Sheba entered the room. She was a white Collie who loved people attention. She zipped around greeting everybody, and paid special attention to Snowball, who was taking her first rest of the day. The two of them were great friends. Sheba ran around Snowball, but couldn't convince her to get to her feet. She gave up on Snowball. Well, there was more than one dog in this playroom. She turned her back on her buddy and trotted away in a huff.

Her huff didn't last long at all. She noticed Sassy was getting some petting, and Sheba certainly couldn't be left out. She came over to Sassy and me, and tried to wriggle her way between us. The Sesame Street episode on In Between was obviously Sheba's favorite. She tried this quite often especially whenever any other dog was getting attention from any counselor. Usually the first dog just headed off to some other activity. Sheba sometimes tried to get in the middle of any two dogs playing together. That never worked. She was either completely ignored or was forced to play with more than one dog at a time.

Once convinced she couldn't control the situation, be it with people or dogs, she just cheerfully dealt with it. Sassy dashed off to seek fun elsewhere. Sheba smushed herself against as many of my body parts as she could reach and was happily wallowing in the individual attention. When Chris, my counselor partner that day, came in Sheba had to race over to get attention from her. She didn't want to miss anybody.

Diablo, a German Shepherd mix, came in a little later. He was a happy dog, always ready to play. Not only was Diablo a welcome sight in camp, we counselors were also happy to see Diablo's mom come in. Several times, she showed up not only with Diablo but also with homemade cookies for us. These were greatly appreciated by the staff. Since Diablo usually checked in during the morning session, I was never quite sure if any of his mom's cookies made it to the afternoon shift. Probably not. Shame on us.

Diablo wasted no time. He was immediately running over everybody, including Chris and me, and swiping whatever ball he could from whoever had one. This rarely caused any friction, which is good because Diablo, once he got hold of a toy, refused to give it up voluntarily. He'd much rather somebody try to pull it away.

He loved to play Just Try to Take My Ball, but his idea of the game was to push the ball into your thigh, daring you to try and take it from him, which, of course, we never did. We all knew how Diablo was with a ball. You simply did not want your fingers anywhere close to his teeth. He was never aggressive with counselors or other dogs. It was just how he played. He never tried to bite, but he did adjust his grip on the ball and a very quick adjustment it was. I saw him coming, the ball in his teeth and aimed at my thigh. I tried to move my hand out of harm's way before he reached me, but not quite fast enough. Diablo hit me, adjusting his grip on the ball at the same time.

"Ouch! Boy-howdy, Diablo. You got me a good one."

Diablo's grip adjustment included a chomp on my finger. This did some real damage and I had a perfect tooth hole at the base of a fingernail. It hurt like the dickens and it was bleeding rather a lot, as fingers tend to do. I left Chris in the playroom while I headed out to do a little first aid. This was painful but purely accidental. It was a case of a dog behaving like a dog, and had absolutely nothing aggressive about it. I just needed to be quicker. Or not play ball with Diablo. Na-a-a-h. I just needed to be quicker.

I got sterilized and bandaged and went back into the playroom. Oh, Yippee. Just in time.

"Excuse me, dogs. Make room for the mop lady. Thank you very much. Anyone else want to add to the puddle while I have the mop handy?"

In came Scally, the Husky, and Wags, the Basenji mix. While Scally paid his respects to the others, Wags followed along, barking his way around the room. Scally brought a ball over for me to throw, which I did. Diablo dropped the ball he already had and raced Scally to see who could get the new ball first. Wags ran after them both, barking all the while. Wags spent almost all most of his camp time barking. Here I had thought this might be a quiet day.

"Look, everybody, Lady's here."

Lady was a German Shorthair mix who was a very lovey dog. She loved people attention and got along well with everybody in the dog world. She never initiated play, but she did run around with everybody, and gladly joined in on most any game in progress. She almost always minded her manners. The exception to her lady-like behavior was that she also just happened to be a pickpocket. If there was the tiniest bit of anything sticking out of a pocket—a tissue, a pen, your keys—Lady would help herself to it. She was so gentle you didn't even know what had happened. Fagin would have loved her.

When she was ready to be petted, which was often, she would approach the nearest counselor and place her head under the counselor's hand and push it up. Really subtle hint. After her first pet of the day, Lady decided to get into the ball game and off she went.

As Chris left the room for her morning break, Rambo arrived. He was pretty friendly for him. He actually came over to greet me. He greeted Lady and Snowball. He ran with Diablo for just a few minutes. He checked in with George and got barked at by Wags and Sheba. He zoomed around with Sassy and Scally for a minute. Boy, he must have had a big bowl of happy cereal that morning. Then he plodded his way over to the front doors and stretched out. After all this rare activity, he must have been tired. Oh, yes, he had definitely worn himself out and wasn't even working on his normal excavating project.

Uh-oh. A major accident at the far end of the room. This would require the mop, the scooper, and the whole mop bucket. I collected all the necessary equipment from the corner and headed down the room.

As I finished up, I turned around and got a major surprise. My nine dogs seem to have dwindled down to only four. George was still in the room, looking a little confused. Snowball was in her corner, resting yet again. Lady and Sheba were looking at the kitchen door.

Hey! That door was open. What the heck? Somebody had opened that door, and I knew darned well it hadn't been me. Maybe I hadn't left that door open when we found the dogs in the kitchen.

I went into the kitchen and there were Scally, Wags, Sassy, Rambo, and Diablo, all very curious about the food, treats, and extra toys stored in there. They were reveling in their adventure in freedom. I collected my truants and hustled them back into the playroom. They didn't argue at all, but I could almost hear them chuckling about their adventure. I was left with a mystery that needed solving. We obviously had a door-opener in the group, but who? No one 'fessed up.

The dogs all went back to doing regular dog stuff. Snowball was still in her corner. Sassy was curled up on a bridge step. Diablo, Scally, and Wags were ripping around the room after each other. George was getting himself into position to do his shoulder slam into Scally. Rambo was now busy trying to excavate the floor at the front doors. Lady was honoring me by placing her head under my hand again. Sheba, not wanting to be ignored, trotted over and tried to wedge herself between us. We convinced her she really could get petted at the same time as another dog, even if she didn't manage to get herself in the middle. Sheba settled for that.

Chris came back and I told her about the escape attempt. We were both keeping a watchful eye on the door, hoping to catch the door-opening critter. Not a single one of them went anywhere close to that door the rest of the morning.

The pre-lunch vigil started and all the dogs were paying very close attention to the kitchen. The dogs were taken, one at a time, out of the playroom and through the elimination station. We always hoped the dogs would make use of this room for its intended purpose. Then they were taken back to their crates. Scally and Wags, almost always rowdy, actually cooperated and headed back to the crate area with no fuss. Snowball was already in the appropriate crate. Diablo wagged his way back to his crate. Sassy and Sheba went in theirs, as did George. Lady voluntarily entered her crate.

It was Rambo's turn. This time he was a little more cooperative. He didn't plant his immovable self, requiring someone to lift him into the crate. He might have been a little easier to move this time, but he still wouldn't go in voluntarily. None of us had been happy with the wheelbarrow method we used last time so we needed to try something else.

The large crates ran about four feet by six feet and floor to ceiling. This was good for big dogs. It was also good for counselors since one could stand upright inside. Memories of the Scally/Wags door-breaking incident prompted me to get into Rambo's crate myself.

I got to the very back of the crate and gently tugged on his lead, sweet-talking him all the while. He eventually succumbed to my charms or maybe he just wanted to be rid of me and stepped in. The next trick was for me to step over and around him, shortening the lead as he got further inside the crate. I maneuvered my way toward the door.

Okay. Rambo was finally inside his crate. I was finally outside of his crate and all of my body parts were still intact. This was good.

So far, none of the dogs had admitted opening that playroom door. Nobody snitched on anybody else. It was a furry wall of silence. Just who was it that had opened that door?

Hm-m-m-m-m....

~ A Snowball Meltdown ~

One day it looked like it really would be a fairly quiet day. I had a ten o'clock start time and, when I arrived, I gave Snowball a pat on her head. Her mom, a fellow counselor, had dropped her off before school that day and would not be working until later in the afternoon. Sassy, Sheba, and George came in and by ten-thirty it looked like every dog that would be in camp was already there.

Kate joined us in the playroom. She dearly loved all the dogs, and all the dogs loved her right back. After greeting the three active dogs, Kate went over to the corner to say hello to Snowball, already sprawled out in rest mode. Kate stretched out on the floor, head to head with Snowball, and took the dog's face in her hands.

"Snowball, are you in there?" Snowball lifted one eye-lid, moved her head just a tad and went back to dreaming her doggy dreams. After forty winks, she was off and running around again. Kate was also off and running again, attending to one of her never-ending duties.

George, the Sharpei, dropped in. George was friendly enough, but not one to seek attention. However, this day, he came right over to say hello. This was really unusual. He normally didn't want much to do with any of the counselors, but here he was actually giving me a friendly greeting and wanting some petting. I was impressed. I mentioned this to Chris, the other counselor on duty. She responded, but I didn't really hear what she told me. I was just happy to have George enjoying my attention for a change.

Mostly Maggie at Doggy Day Camp

After about half an hour, when Chris heard me call George by name, she repeated what she'd told me earlier. "Barb, that isn't George. This is a new dog named Buddy."

Oh. That explained the friendliness. I hadn't met Buddy before. I wondered how long it would take to tell the two apart just by looking at them, if they were in the room together. I was sure there would be some subtle differences in looks, but they were never at camp at the same time so I never found out. I knew I'd be able to distinguish them by personality, though.

Oh-oh, here came Spike, a very active Weimaraner. Spike absolutely loved to tear around the room with other dogs or all by himself. He was never still. He would deign to let you pet him once in a while, but he usually didn't have the time for such frivolities. Spike was definitely a mover and a shaker in the dog world.

Sassy and Sheba were busy climbing all over each other. Buddy went over to invite Spike to a game of Run Rampant and Bark. Spike got into the game with gusto. He was zooming all over the room, barking about every six feet or so. Buddy was trying his darnedest to keep up and barking about every ten feet or so. Snowball was restless. She didn't want to play, and she wasn't lying down. It wasn't likely that the barking would upset her. That was common in camp. Well, this was odd.

There were workmen up on the roof directly overhead. This might account for Snowball's nervous behavior. They were making a lot of noise, and Snowball apparently didn't like it. She got on top of the bridge, an extremely rare thing for her to do. The noise increased, and Snowball became more and more agitated. She got off the bridge, but got right back up again. She was really whining and literally shaking now. Snowball was the most laid-back dog I'd ever seen. Nothing bothered her. This behavior came as a complete surprise.

I went over to the bridge to calm her down. I talked to her and hugged her, but it simply wasn't working. Chris tried to calm her too and had no success either. Poor Snowball. She was rapidly coming unglued. Her favorite person in the world was not in the building. We had to think of some way to help her. Putting her in a crate wouldn't work since she would then be both isolated and confined, with the noise level just as high in there. Chris and I were fresh out of ideas. I got on the walkie-talkie and paged Kate who came back to see what the problem was. We knew she'd come up with a solution.

She came in and tried to calm Snowball. This worked for her as well as it had worked for Chris and me. Kate was working in the front office and the thumping and scraping were not quite as loud in there. She suggested that Snowball go with her. We agreed that this was the only option available. Snowball was put on a lead and the two of them headed up front. Snowball, however, was so distraught that the only place she wanted to be was out of the building altogether. Kate took her out for a short walk to get her mind off all the scary racket. After a few minutes, Snowball calmed down enough that she could come back into the store without totally freaking out. She stayed close to Kate in the front office for the duration.

While Snowball was out of the playroom, the remainder of the dogs kept busy. Sassy started a game of Nip and Hide with Spike, who thought this was the grandest game he'd ever played. Chris and I were both mindful of our knees. We did have to break the two up now and then, but it wasn't too bad, considering the determination of Sassy and the size and rowdiness of Spike. Their energy levels were about as high as the noise level.

Buddy and Sheba entered into a race, which kept them busy for a fair amount of time. When the race ended, they both headed over to Chris and I, one dog each, for some affection.

About an hour and a half later, the workers left. Quiet having been restored, Kate brought Snowball back into the playroom where Sassy, Sheba, Spike, and Buddy had been playing the entire time, paying no attention at all to the noises overhead.

They warmly welcomed her back and Sheba invited her to join in a race around the room. Sounded like a good idea to Snowball and the two of them were off and running. Sassy, Spike, and Buddy were playing Tuggie. Sheba and Snowball raced around the room until Snowball got tired. Sheba came over to be petted and Snowball plopped herself down in her favorite corner to get a belly-rub.

It had been a stressful couple of hours for our Snowball. None of us had ever seen our calm and mellow den mother upset over anything.

Once those scary noises were gone, though, they were totally forgotten. It was back to business as usual, and Snowball was back to normal.

Even the calmest personality can occasionally get stressed.

~ Excitement in the Small Room ~

The small playroom, about one third the size of the bigger room, was much more private. There was a door with an upper half window between the small room and the kennel area. This was the door most often used. In the back corner of the room was an emergency exit door. A double Dutch door separated the two playrooms. This provided an extra exit from either room. The top half of the double door was usually left open, which tended to open up the smaller room, primarily for the comfort of the counselors.

While there were usually anywhere from seven to twelve dogs in the big room, there were seldom more than three or four dogs in the small room on the rare occasion the small room was in use at all. Ninety-five percent of the time all the dogs were in the large playroom. Most of the small dogs who came in on a regular basis ended up having a great time in with the bigger, more active dogs. Occasionally, though, we had dogs, big and small, come in who didn't do well with the rowdy bunch in the bigger playroom. We would put these quiet ones into the adjoining smaller playroom, where they were more comfortable.

My own sixty-pound Toby was one of these. He was old and was having trouble with both his hearing and his vision. He didn't care much for camp and only attended a couple of times. He didn't have an aggressive bone in his body, and he put up with being there, but he was much happier to stay home and snooze on his own bed while I was gone. There was also a large three-legged Briard who preferred the company of the calmer and less rowdy dogs.

While the smaller playroom was for the less active campers, it was not without amenities. For a little interest and to give the small room dogs something to climb on, there was a playhouse with open doors and windows and a second level that was about twenty inches high. There were several toys in this room even though these quiet campers rarely used them.

On an average day in this room, the most excitement was if all of the little ones tried to get out the door at the same time someone was coming in or going out. Even then, this rush for the door was generally more exciting for the counselors than it was for the dogs. The small room dogs were not nearly as energetic as the big room dogs, but that didn't mean they didn't have their own adventures.

Queenie, a Miniature Pinscher, and quite a wallflower, came to camp every now and then. She was a nervous little thing and there was no question about where she would be most comfortable.

One morning Bonnie and Clyde came in to keep Queenie company, as did Duchess and Cedric. This was a very quiet group, and I knew they wouldn't bother Queenie. Sparky had just come in. She was a long-haired Dachshund who had the most beautiful ears ever seen on a dog. They were a very warm reddish-brown color, running to black around the edges. They were long and silky and shiny. Shoot, I would have paid Bonnie, my furry little hairdresser, big bucks if she could have colored my hair just like Sparky's gorgeous ears.

Sparky was one feisty, but gentle, little lady. She played with the big dogs most of the time, dashing around the room, under the bridge, on top of the bridge, getting her pets whenever she could stand still, which wasn't very often. She got along well with all the dogs. I thought she would be a good one to try to get the others in the small room to play.

Boy, did she try. Bonnie ran around with her for a few minutes. Clyde, of course, barked at this. Duchess was on guard, watching the bottom of the door, and ignored Sparky completely. Cedric watched from the second level of the playhouse. Sparky joined him and he actually returned her greeting. For the most part, though, my quiet little group ignored her. It was clear that Sparky would rather be in with the active dogs. So, she and I headed in the direction of the big room.

Before we made it to the double Dutch door, we were greeted by an apparition sailing over it. It was Casper in flying mode. Casper was aptly named. He was a white German Shepherd mix with ice-blue eyes that gave him an eerie appearance. He was a handsome dog with only one vice. He was a jumper. On the counters, over the counter, wherever he wanted to be. Now here he came, Casper the Ghost dog at his flying best. I was very happy that my little charges were along the walls or in the playhouse and not in the middle of the room. I did not want them to be landing pads for Casper.

As soon as his feet hit the floor, I zipped right over to him, not quite sure what he would do next. I also wasn't quite sure what the little dogs would do. He sure had everyone's attention. Casper just looked around. What he saw was a bunch of startled little dogs and one stunned counselor. The little dogs just looked at him looking around at them.

"Sorry, Casper, there will be no more flying today."

I convinced good ol' Casper that he really needed to go back to his own room, through the doors and not over them. He was more than happy to oblige. I'm sure we looked like a pretty boring bunch by his standards. Back to the big room he went and Sparky tagged along.

As I let the two dogs into the big playroom, I saw quite a sight. Kate was sitting on the floor and Maggie was sitting on her lap. At least I thought it was Kate. All I could see was one leg from the knee down and an arm and a hand up close to Maggie's head. Had to be Kate. She was the only one at camp who was small enough to disappear that completely under Maggie. After some convincing, Maggie got to her feet, and Kate stood up, laughing. We all agreed that there would be no more lap-sitting for Maggie. She's just too big and we sure couldn't have anyone ending up squashed flatter than a fritter.

After the Kate and Maggie show, I closed both the top and bottom of the Dutch door. My little group relaxed, happy to return to doing nothing and secure in the knowledge that there would be no more big, scary dogs flying in. This had been a fairly exciting morning for the little dogs. They had taken it all in stride, though, even nervous little Queenie.

Quiet time with quiet dogs is soothing to the soul.

~ Inside Out ~

Most of the animal activity in the store was not visible from the camp area. This was a good thing because bunnies, mice, guinea pigs, and ferrets would certainly attract unwanted attention from the canine campers. The glass doors separating the store from the camp would be mobbed with very excited dogs trying to figure out how to get out there and play with all these enticing little critters. Definitely not conducive to keeping dogs calm.

I rarely went directly back to the camp area when I arrived at work. I would give the manager a shout to let her know I was in. Then I had to wish a good morning to the small furry animals, the rats and the mice. Then it was over to the birds. I checked in with the fish, the snakes, and lizards. I even took a look at the—shudder—creepy-crawly tarantulas and scorpions.

I actually liked the lizards and the snakes. Some of them had gorgeous markings. Contrary to popular opinion, they are not slimy at all. Their skin is kind of cool and dry to the touch. When I first started working in camp, I passed by a snake aquarium and inside was a freshly shed skin - whole and intact. It was such a fascinating skin that I decided my five-year-old grandson would like to see it. I asked the snake lady if I could have it. She thought it was a rather strange request but took it out and boxed it up for me. My grandson was impressed when I presented it to him. My daughter and my granddaughter, however, were not quite as thrilled.

Okay, time to 'fess up. Animal lover that I am, I am not the world's biggest fan of spiders, scorpions, centipedes, or millipedes. In fact, these things give me the heebie-jeebies. However, the Spider Guy who worked with the creepy things challenged me repeatedly to hold a Tarantula. He told me he would get it out of its aquarium home and put it in the palm of my hand. It took me months, but I finally worked up the courage and agreed to hold one. Was I nuts? Maybe.

I was expecting him to get out one of the giant, hairy things. You know, the kind of spider that can drag off your children and/or your Irish Wolfhound. Was that what I ended up with? No. He told me to hold out my hand, palm up and parallel to the floor. He placed this slender, skinny-legged, hairless, and plug ugly female tarantula on my hand, warning me not to drop her because she would explode and die if she fell to the floor. Was he kidding me? I didn't know for sure, but I would try not to jerk my hand and have her fall to the floor. I didn't like the thing, but I didn't want her to explode. So the nasty ol' spider took one step to get all the way across my palm and that was more than enough for me. The guy was laughing at me as he put the spider back in the tank. Then he suggested I hold a scorpion.

"Not on your life, Spider Guy."

Being out of sight of the camp crew during this little adventure was a good thing. I knew everybody at work would hear about it, but I was glad they couldn't see me cringing and making faces when I had that icky spider on my palm. As soon as I reached the camp I made instant use of the closest sanitizing hand cleaner dispensers.

One early morning, just inside the camp lobby, I found a chameleon. I don't have any idea how he'd escaped his aquarium, how he'd managed to get inside the camp area, or how long he'd been there. Fortunately no dogs had come in yet, so he hadn't been the object of canine curiosity. He had to be freezing and really did need to be in his warm aquarium. I told the lizard lady about him. I'm sure she thought I was afraid to touch him myself. Not so. I tend to have rather shaky hands, and I just didn't want to risk hurting him if my hands took on a life of their own when I was trying to get hold of him. He was very small. Lizard lady came back and took him back to his own cozy place. I'm sure he was much more comfortable there.

The dogs did pay some attention to people passing by the window, but not much. Well, except for Maggie and Snowball who deemed it their duty to bark fiercely at everybody. This was generally a short-term activity, though, and they would go back to the gang after sufficiently scaring the bejeebers out of the folks beyond the glass.

The entire door had been left uncovered when camp first started. We discovered very quickly that passing dogs, out shopping with the family, would send the entire camp into a barking frenzy. Thankfully, the bottom half of the glass was now covered. Once in a while, one of our taller campers would spot a doggy shopper out there and go a little nuts. Most of the time the campers wouldn't stay at the window long at all. They had better things to do.

Every now and then a shopper would hold his little dog up so he could see the camp dogs happily playing together and running around the playroom. That would create quite a stir with the campers. When this happened, one of us would step out and ask the person to take their little dog away from the window to avoid mass hysteria inside the camp. The people never took offense at this and put their dog down pretty quick. Then they would often ask questions about the camp program. We, of course, encouraged them to bring their dog in for evaluation if they thought the camp would be fun for their pet.

We saw the occasional errant Robin or Sparrow inside the store. They flitted about the store for a day or two until they eventually made their way back out the front door. Because they were small and tended to stay up high, most of the dogs didn't even realize they were there.

Wild Mallards zipping around high and low, on the other hand, were not so easy to ignore. One fine day, a pair of them just quietly waddled into the store. They got panicky and took flight, sending the entire staff into a tizzy. A couple of the campers spotted them flying past the camp doors. They both landed just outside the doors, waddling around in plain sight of the dogs. The tizzy of the staff was greatly dwarfed by the tizzy of the dogs. Good grief.

Maggie went berserk. She was up on her back paws, front paws as high as she could get them on the window, pounding the glass and barking for all she was worth. As long as there was a duck in view, there was no way she was leaving her spot at the window. Snowball gave a couple of mighty barks, but soon lost interest.

Luckily for those of us in the playroom, the ducks decided they preferred the front of the store to the barking frenzy emanating from the camp and disappeared from view. Out of sight, out of mind definitely held true for the campers. Whew. Store staffers finally managed to scoot the ducks back outside.

The camp lobby was also the lobby for the grooming section. The camp dogs could see into the lobby and they tended to get temporarily excited when dogs came in for any reason. Once a dog had gone on into the grooming area across the lobby from camp, the campers instantly put that dog out of mind.

I was in the playroom one morning when one of the other counselors came into the room. "Hey," she said. "Did you see the walrus in grooming?"

A walrus? Ri-i-i-ght. You would think I'd have noticed a walrus. I mean, a walrus would have been darned hard to miss. I scoffed, sure she was pulling my leg. Chris suggested I go over and take a look while she covered the playroom. Well, maybe I'd had my attention focused elsewhere. Naturally I couldn't resist my curiosity and to grooming I went.

My goodness. There, being bathed, was a huge mountain of a dog. I had never seen a dog like this one and had no idea what kind of dog he was. He was a dark shade of grey with huge jowls and a few wrinkles in his coat. I could see why Chris had referred to him as a walrus. The person bathing him was his handler so I asked about the dog. It was a Neapolitan Mastiff who was going to enter the area dog show early the next morning, for which he had to be clean as possible. That dog was definitely impressive. I know I was certainly impressed.

Cats also came in for grooming, which did not interest the campers at all. Cats came in via carriers so the dogs never saw them. Counselors did see them. There was a gorgeous long-haired cat on the table. He was obviously not the most cooperative animal. The groomer was almost done, but asked if someone could come over and hold onto the cat so she could finish his underside. Over I went.

This was not a happy cat, and my holding his front paws to keep him still was not improving his disposition. Between the groomer working quickly and me holding onto the poor thing, that cat's grooming was done before she could get angry enough to strike out at us. That was definitely good.

Men working on the ceiling lights were a short-lived, but major attraction. The hydraulic scaffolding they used seemed to hold some fascination for the campers. They didn't bark. They didn't jump on the windows. They just watched. They looked like they were wondering why these particular humans were going up and down instead of staying on the floor where humans were supposed to be. They didn't ponder this phenomenon for long. It became boring rather quickly. So it was back to playing.

Mom or Dad coming to pick up the camper was, without a doubt, the most exciting thing that a camp dog could see through the windows. They couldn't wait to plant a few affectionate slurps on the faces of those they most loved. The first time or two the dogs were in camp, they paid not one whit of attention to the counselor once they spotted their people. This was an important time to make use of the slip-lead. We had to pull the dogs away from Happy Pet Parent at the window. When this happened, the dogs assumed they were being dog-napped and would never see their people again. This did not make them happy.

After a few days and a suggestion from the counselors, Mom or Dad realized it was best not to grin and wave like crazy at their pooch from the far side of the window. Regular campers always seemed to sense when it was about time for their people to come. They geared up for leaving. It didn't take long for these dogs to figure out that if they listened to the counselors, they would get to see Mom or Dad in short order even though they'd been having fun all day with their camp buddies.

There's no place like home.

~ Stuff Happens ~

There was just no way camp could ever be boring. There was always something unexpected lurking just around the corner. Some of these unexpected events could be attributed to the dogs, but some could be attributed to not-always-brilliant actions of staff members. And sometimes stuff just happened.

* * * *

We found, even before camp opened to the public, we could expect the unexpected. One morning, Snowball was with her mom in the small playroom. There was an emergency exit in the corner of the room and Snowball took a notion to jump up on it. To our surprise it flew open and Snowball was out that door like a shot. Fortunately, she was a well-trained dog and immediately came back at the first command. The very next day that door was fixed so that no dog could just push it open. While the small room seldom contained exceptionally large dogs, that door had been a safety/security hazard.

* * * *

One day when Maggie arrived, she barely greeted Snowball. That was highly unusual behavior for her. She was always anxious to greet other campers. The reason she was so quiet soon became obvious.

After the first Maggie clean-up, the other counselor and I thought she might not be feeling well. After two more major clean-ups within fifteen minutes it was clear she really was having digestive problems of epic proportions. We couldn't keep her at camp. We took her back to her crate and called to have her mom pick her up. Poor Maggie continued to have problems while she waited to be picked up. Her crate was a disaster.

Once Maggie had gone home, it was up to me to clean and sanitize that crate. Thankfully it was solid on three sides, keeping any mess from adjoining crates. I hooked up the hose and got busy scrubbing it down. There were drainage ditches at the back of these large kennels so it wasn't as horrendous a job as it could have been.

* * * *

Very early one morning I was busy with my routine to get ready for the day. I was surprised to see Maggie in the camp lobby with her person. I was more surprised when the woman told me there was no check-in desk and no receptionist at the front doors to the store. I checked Maggie in and took her back to the kennel.

When I got back to the lobby, there was Norton, a deaf Cocker spaniel. Still no sign of our receptionist. I checked Norton in and took him back to his crate.

Norton was a real sweetheart, who didn't play much at all. Because he was deaf, he received a lot of petting. To get Norton's attention you had to touch him, sometimes even if he was looking right at you. All the counselors were pretty good at Norton Sign Language. He managed very well in spite of this handicap. I think he must have been able to feel vibrations in the floor and on the climbing toys. He was never caught up in the doggy mayhem going on all around him. He spent most of his time on the top of the bridge, quietly watching the pandemonium. He did occasionally set up a howl that could be heard over everything. There didn't seem to be any reason for this. He just did it. At those times it was necessary to get right down in front of him and assure him all was well in Dogdom. After some petting and reassurance, he would quiet down 'til the next time.

Back out in the lobby, I was stunned to find four more unrelated dogs waiting for me. It was highly unusual for more than three dogs to arrive at camp at the same time and, most often, two of the three were dogs that lived together. Still no sign of a receptionist, but Kerri, our operations manager, was in the lobby She didn't look happy.

No wonder. Our receptionist had just called to tell Kerri she wouldn't be in that day or any other. She'd quit. Kerri said she would call one of the other counselors and have her come in right away. Given the number of dogs piling up, I thought that was a good idea.

Kerri went off to make her call, and I got busy checking in the four waiting dogs. All four had decided it must be play time already since they were all together in a common area. I worked as quickly as I could, untangling leashes that were wound around dogs, their people, and me.

By the time the other counselor arrived, the flurry of check-ins had abated. The portable front-desk never made it to the front that day.

* * * *

Within the first couple of weeks of camp opening, Kate and I were in the playroom with Maggie. No other campers had arrived yet. I thought it would be fun to sprawl out with Maggie. Kate and I both knew full well that this was something frowned on by our teacher, but I told Kate I simply couldn't resist.

I stretched out on the floor and invited Maggie to join me. She did. There we were, side by side on the floor. I threw an arm across her and gave her a belly-rub. Maggie was quite content with the affectionate attention.

After just a few minutes, I got back up .or tried to get up. I made it to my hands and knees. Maggie stood up and planted her two huge front paws on the middle of my back. I was in an awkward position with all that weight on my back. It only took a little verbal convincing from Kate and me to get Maggie to put all four feet back on the floor. Well, now I knew why we weren't supposed to do that. I was glad I'd done it, but I never felt compelled to do it again.

* * * *

There were three counselors and three dogs in the larger playroom one afternoon. Woofy, a black and white Chow mix was there. He was a laid-back kind of guy who never got into mischief. There was Charlie, a really big brown Doberman, also laid-back personality-wise. Both of these dogs were rare visitors at camp. George, the Sharpei was at camp periodically and he was the third dog. Things were going along well. Charlie and George were playing with each other. Woofy was sitting and watching.

Mostly Maggie at Doggy Day Camp

Out of the blue, for some reason known only to the dog, Charlie got a little annoyed with George and made a determined effort to bite him. He quickly tried again. This was absolutely unacceptable behavior.

The slip leads we all had were instantly put on all three dogs. One counselor moved George out of harm's way. The second counselor pulled Charlie back at the same time. Unfortunately, this move put him close to poor Woofy, who was just sitting quietly, not bothering anybody. We all saw it coming.

Charlie took aim, but the counselors were quicker. Poor Woofy. This scared him. Charlie was now pulled back in the opposite direction so I was able to tug Woofy out of Charlie's reach. It took him a few minutes, but he pulled himself together.

Charlie was taken out of the playroom. His behavior was very unusual and surprised us all. His attack had been very fast and, as far as any of we counselors could tell, was completely unprovoked. Even though no damage was done, it was a serious enough offense that we three counselors agreed he could be a danger to other dogs and to counselors. Charlie was expelled from camp.

* * * *

One morning, Snowball's mom decided it was time for Snowball to have a treat. She went into the playroom and gave Snowball her treat. Unfortunately, three other dogs were about to come into the playroom as well. In they came.

Immediately discovering there was a yummy goodie in the room, they went after it. Snowball let them know in no uncertain terms this particular munchie was hers and hers alone. This differs from food aggression because the treat was in shared territory. It was not the normal time for food and was, therefore, a bonus. To the other dogs, this meant they had just as much right to it as Snowball. Snowball and her treat were taken out of the playroom and crisis was averted.

* * * *

Yes, things occasionally got off-track. We always managed to get back on in short order.

Stuff happens. You learn

~ All Dogs Like Me ~

My family has always teased me about my love for animals. They would tell me that all small children and all animals like me. They're either too young or too dumb to know better. In this case, the teasing had some merit. All small children and animals really do like me.

If they don't take a shine to me instantly, we become buddies within the first two minutes of our meeting. A customer was coming into the store as I was leaving one day. She had two Italian Greyhounds with her, and I, naturally, asked if I could pet them. She said yes, and I immediately dropped to my knees to be at their level.

The lady was about to say something more when her two little greys zipped over to me and I was petting them both. The lady was stunned. She told me one of the two was extremely nervous around people, a regular "spook" that would normally cower behind her person rather than meet someone new. Now, here they both were, enjoying the whole petting thing. I never did discover which of the two the shy one was. I did feel rather privileged that whichever one it was, allowed me to touch her. All dogs really do like me. Everybody knows that.

I had a late start time one morning, and Quentin, an American Bulldog, was already in the playroom and having a great time. He was running with the other dogs. He was getting his pets from the counselor on duty. Then he sat down on the counselor's feet, a sign of affection, I was told. I hadn't met him yet, but he certainly seemed friendly. He looked like a happy, fun-loving dog, that is, until I went into the playroom.

Usually the dogs would all come over to say good morning, and they did that day. All of them except Quentin. Not only did he not want to meet me, he was audibly growling a rather serious growl at me and was backing away. This was a new experience. The back-pedaling made the growling seem not quite so threatening. It was just enough to make me pause.

I had been asked at my second interview if I was afraid of dogs. I told management I am not afraid of dogs, but I do respect them, no matter their size. An American Bulldog is big enough and powerful enough to demand respect. His growl, added to his size, commanded it. I took Quentin's warning very seriously.

I stopped moving for just a few seconds, not quite sure of my strategy. I decided the best thing I could do was to go ahead with my regular routine. I wouldn't pester Quentin, but I didn't want him to think I wasn't in charge, either. For most of that morning we kept a watchful eye on each other and gave each other plenty of space. I did call him by name and talked to him like I talked to all the dogs, but I didn't pay any special attention to him, and I didn't try to pet him.

It was getting late in the morning and Quentin still wouldn't approach me. I ended up resorting to bribery. I went into the kitchen and gathered some treats for all the dogs. Quentin did take a treat from me. He grabbed it and ran off, but at least he took the treat. I was really pleased he had left every single one of my fingers with me, intact and still attached to my hand. I saw that as progress.

So, what was the deal with Quentin? Maybe I reminded him of someone in his life who wasn't particularly nice to him. Whatever the reason, there was just no getting around it. He did not like me. Until I met Quentin, such a thing was inconceivable. The story that a dog didn't like me moved through the store like wild-fire.

Dogs like me. Everyone in the store knew that. We all kind of wondered what would happen the next day. Would Quentin decide I was okay after all? Would Quentin spend another day in camp avoiding me? Would Quentin do me some serious hurt if given the opportunity? Ah-h-h, the stuff of a good soap opera.

The next morning, we started all over again. Quentin was about to go into the building at the same time I was approaching it. He spotted me and started barking like crazy and lunging at me, pulling like mad on his lead. His owner and I decided that, even though I was right there and available, someone else should take Quentin back to the kennel area. I waited outside for a couple of minutes to give Quentin time to get back to the camp.

Once in the playroom, things eased up a little. He was still pretty wary, but he wasn't barking, growling, or lunging at me. He didn't run away from me either. After an hour or so he even let me pat his head once or twice. Things were definitely improving. By noon good ol' Quentin was not threatening me at all. To my surprise and delight, he was actually approaching me on his own. I didn't have to bribe him any more. Then, would you believe this? Quentin came and sat down next to my feet, not on them, but close enough. It was a good sign.

I found out later that even other store locations had heard about it. Shortly after the Quentin incident several employees from several of our stores went to work at the local dog show, and. I was stunned to hear from people I had never met they had heard there was a dog who didn't like me. I guess I had a good dog reputation. Dogs really do like me. It's true. It just took Quentin a little longer to figure that out.

Quentin and I were never together in camp again, but I like to think we were on our way to being buddies.

Sometimes acquaintances take a little time and effort to make it as far as friendship.

~ Houdini Dogs Identified ~

Aha. The mystery had been solved. We finally identified who the door-opening escape artists were. The culprits were caught red-pawed. Turned out we had two door openers among the campers. Scally was one of them. He only had to put his weight on the lever and barely wiggle his paw to open the door. Sassy, who actually had to stretch to lean on the lever and throw her body slightly backwards to open it, was the other. Hm-m-m-m … Sassy had been one of dogs we found in the kitchen the day the door had been found opened. I suspect she had opened it but I'll never know for sure.

Once we knew who was responsible, when either Scally or Sassy was in the playroom, a lightweight portable fence was placed across the Dutch door to the kitchen. Flimsy as this fence was, most of the dogs wanted nothing to do with it.

Door openers were not the only ones who occasionally made good an escape out of the playroom and into the secured kitchen area. While Scally and Sassy were the ones that actually opened the door, it in no way meant they were the only two dogs who took advantage of that open door. If any of the doors remained open and undetected by the counselors, even for a second, most of the dogs thought it was a challenge to see how far they could explore before being hustled back into the playroom.

Cedric was a pro at scooting out. His method was simple. Wait until a taller dog (which could have been almost any other camp dog) was being taken out for whatever reason and just run along under that dog. Hugging the floor to avoid radar detection did work once in a while, but he didn't get out often and he never got far. He was always caught immediately, and he always cooperated when directed back into the playroom, chuckling under his breath along the way, I'm sure.

Then, of course, there was Casper. He simply flew out of where he didn't want to be and flew in to where he did want to be. His method of escape was effective only once, and then only as far as the smaller room.

Casper's attempts to fly out were not unique. Both Maggie and Diablo had been known to consider it a time or two. It never worked for them. They took far too much time preparing to launch and always got busted before they got airborne.

The most surprising near-escape ever, though, was completely unintentional. It was a ten o'clock start for me that day. I went directly into the large playroom and greeted the several dogs that were already there, including Maggie. The other counselor left for her break.

Just after she left, a woman customer came up to the break-away glass doors that separated the camp from the store. Maggie, as expected, zoomed over to see who it was, barking her big bark on her way. This startled the woman, causing her to jump back a bit. Maggie, as expected, jumped up to slap her paws on the door, causing the woman to back up a bit further. I was right behind Maggie, ready to pull her away from the windows.

"WHOA!"

Maggie's feet hit the glass and both doors flew open. My eyes got huge and my jaw dropped clear down to the floor. The customer had the same reaction. I knew Maggie wouldn't intentionally hurt the woman on the other side, but at more than one hundred twenty pounds, Maggie could very easily have knocked her down and caused serious injury when the lady hit the floor.

That was bad enough, but then my imagination kicked in. It wasn't my life that flashed before my eyes. It wasn't the customer's life that flashed before my eyes. What flashed before my eyes was a vision of Maggie dashing out of the camp and running rampant through the store, wreaking unintentional havoc all the while.

I could envision terrified customers screaming and scattering. I could see cans and bags of dog food flying, dog toys and balls all over the place, and lots of folks slipping and sliding on the debris. I could see innocent little bunnies, mice, guinea pigs, and ferrets cowering in fear as Maggie jumped up on their cages to check them out. I could see parakeets, love birds, and cockatiels going into cardiac arrest. I could see aquariums shattered and flooding the store, fish flopping and gasping on the floor. I could see tarantulas and scorpions cruising around, causing even more panic among the customers and me. I could see Maggie getting more scared by the minute with all the noise and panic she had inadvertently caused. Worse, I could see her heading out the front door of the store, terrified, out into the parking lot on her way to the busy street.

There was no time to use the slip lead I had hanging on my neck. Definitely no time for a walkie-talkie here. I was so stunned I just yelled for help. REAL LOUD.

Thank goodness, Maggie was just as stunned as I was. She hesitated just long enough for me to grab her with one hand and to grab one door with the other. That woman customer was terrific. She had been startled by Maggie's barking, but was not afraid. She stood her ground and grabbed both doors, pushing them closed as soon as I had the entire Maggie back inside the confines of the playroom. I immediately locked the doors. Whichever counselor opened camp that morning had either forgotten to check those doors or thought she was locking it and, instead, had mistakenly unlocked it.

By the time another counselor came into the room, things were back under control. I left the other counselor in charge so I could go out to thank the woman for her help. We decided it was a good thing Maggie had hesitated and we hadn't. We both laughed at the picture we must have made and everything was okay. I ended up taking a break when I hadn't even been at work fifteen minutes yet. As soon as my heart stopped pounding, I headed back to work.

With the help of that calm customer, this unintended escape attempt was stopped before it could become a reality. Since my first day opening camp I was particular about checking door security. After this incident, I began checking all the door locks, no matter what time I started my shift.. I double checked every single door every single time.

Escapes were also a slight possibility when the dogs were excited about getting out of their crates to head back to the playrooms or to be picked up by their people. The bigger dogs were fairly easy to handle. We slipped a lead on them as they came through the crate doors, so we had them under control right away. The smaller dogs were generally on the second level. These guys loved to jump right past you, from about shoulder height to the floor. The trick was to open the door just wide enough to get your hand on the dog, keep your body in front of the opening, and lift the dog out. This was pretty easy and usually worked well for the little dogs. We did realize it wasn't so easy we could let our guard down. We had to be prepared for any escape possibility.

We counselors had our own Houdini methods of getting out of the playroom undetected. It was something we'd had to learn early on. If some of the dogs even suspected a door was about to open, they would zip right over on the off chance they could make it out. If a counselor opened a door without scouting the area, curious dogs, large and small, would make a bee-line for that door. The big ones were fairly easy to catch. You could reach down and stop them with your hand. They didn't seriously want to escape. They just wanted to explore as much as they could.

It was the little guys we really had to watch out for. They were not at a convenient height to just reach down and grab. You couldn't block them with a hip or a thigh. Besides, they were quicker than one would think.

During the first week we were opened, Chris and I were in the smaller playroom. I believe we had more dogs in the room that day than any other day ever. There were seven small campers in the room. They heard me unlatch the door that lead into the kennel area, and they zoomed over before I could make it through the door. Not a one of them stood knee-high and there was a flurry of fur around my ankles.

Did Chris come over and help me scoot the dogs away from the door. No. She was too busy laughing at me to be of any help at all. I finally managed to get through the door without being followed.

It didn't take counselors too long to figure out a plan. If the dogs were close to one door, we went out a different door, quickly and quietly. If the dogs were hovering about, some close to every door, we put our backs to the door, opened it just enough to go through sideways, one leg, ankle or foot blocking the door until we were clear. We didn't have nearly as many escape plans as the dogs, though.

You just have to admire the creativity of the canine mind. It helped that the dogs hesitated now and then.

~ A Soggy Doggy Day ~

Snowball came in one morning, her usual lovable self. She took a look around the room and noticed there were no other dogs yet. This never bothered Snowball in the least. With the exception of the men making noise on the roof, Snowball didn't let anything bother her. She got her morning greeting and plopped herself down in her favorite corner to wait patiently for her pals to arrive. It was a short wait.

A new dog I hadn't met before entered the playroom. Boy, he was a little cutie. He was a black mop of a Cockerpoo named Shorty, and he was just adorable. Snowball got to her feet and lumbered over to greet the little newcomer. She was about ten times his size, but that made no difference to either of them. Snowball and I hadn't been there when Shorty came to camp for the first time. He was new to both of us. Snowball and Shorty hit it off immediately. He was friendly enough with me, but he took a real liking to Snowball, our gentle giant.

Shorty got hold of a ball and invited Snowball to race around with him. She was up for some action. Shorty was a quick little guy who could zoom in and out under the bridge where Snowball couldn't follow. Not to be deterred, Snowball came up with a plan. She waited for Shorty, weighing in at about eleven pounds, to get close to her. When he did, Snowball, all one hundred five pounds of her, very gently took the tip of Shorty's tail in her teeth and hung on. Shorty led the way, running on his short little legs at a pace that was comfortable for Snowball to lope along behind him. They looked for all the world like an odd elephant parade.

After a few laps around the room, Snowball was tuckered out, turned loose of Shorty's tail, and headed back to her corner to sprawl.

Shorty followed her, stretching out on the floor face to face with her. He pushed the ball toward Snowball to entice her, but she didn't take the bait. She put her head down on her paws, intent on taking her rest. Shorty stayed put, quietly and patiently waiting, just watching her, the ball unattended between them. He was genuinely enamored of Snowball.

Duchess and Cedric arrived. Duchess gave Shorty a quick, rather courtly greeting, which he ignored. She took her regular post at the bottom of the door. Cedric didn't even bother to acknowledge Shorty and headed for the top of the bridge. There he stayed, ever on the lookout for his beloved Kate. Shorty stayed right where he was, waiting for his big new friend to get a second breath.

I spotted another new dog entering, another German Shorthair mix. Wow. He sure looked lively. His lady was pretty much stumbling along behind him, hanging on for dear life. One of the other counselors was going to evaluate him, and, if all went well, he would join us in the playroom before long.

Scally and Wags rushed into the playroom. Scally dashed over to check out Shorty. Wags followed him, barking, of course. Shorty barked once in reply, gave up waiting for Snowball, and headed off with Scally. Wags stuck right with them, barking furiously the entire time. This got him a quick water spray. He stopped barking and actually left Scally and decided to play ball with me. As long as his best buddy was in sight, Wags would occasionally get into activities without Scally.

Wags found his ball of choice and brought it over, dropping it at my feet. I already knew his game. Once he dropped the ball, I was to pick it up and throw it for him. We did this a lot. So, as Wags expected, I picked up the ball and tossed it. As I anticipated, he brought it back and dropped it at my feet again. We did this five or six times, just like we'd done from his first day at camp. On the next drop, though, Wags changed the rules on me with no advance notice. I reached down to pick up the ball as usual. Just as my hand was about to touch the ball, Wags made a grab for it.! He had never done this before.

"Ouch!" Oh, no, not again. This time, it was just a little nip on my thumb, a slight scratch with very little blood. Boy, if I was going to continue playing ball with these guys, I really did have to do something about speeding up my reaction time. I knew without a doubt I would continue to play ball with the dogs. I was willing to take my chances.

Off I went for some antiseptic and a band-aid. Like Diablo, this had been an accident. Wags wasn't trying to bite me. I did the first aid routine and went back into the playroom. I gave Wags a pat and everything was fine.

The evaluation of the new dog was finished. He'd made it this far and it was time for him to meet the rest of the dogs. He was placed in the portable fence enclosure inside the playroom. Snowball was let into the enclosure and the two dogs checked each other out. Mellow Snowball was the dog of choice for this duty no matter who the newcomer was. Counselors were all close by and alert to any adverse reaction. There was none. This was one friendly dog. His name was Boomer, a fitting name for a most happy and rowdy dog.

Boomer sniffed, wiggled, and wagged like crazy at Snowball. The rest of the campers, including Duchess and Cedric, had crowded around outside the fence, trying to get close to the new guy. Boomer worked his way along the fence checking them all out, tail happily wagging furiously the whole way. Well, he sure wasn't at all shy, and he was thrilled to meet everybody, counselors included.

He and Snowball were released to join the others in the playroom. Now all the dogs were crowding around Boomer, sniffing like mad. He took it all in stride and sniffed everybody right back. There was no doubt that Boomer was a major player in the dog world. It took him only a couple of minutes to make himself at home. Then they were all off and running. What a happy-go-lucky dog he was. He just seemed to love life. Boomer would liven the place up a bit. As if we needed livening up in the big playroom.

Boomer went face to face with Scally and Wags. He was already a regular after only a short time in new surroundings. Scally went to one side of the bridge, followed by Wags, who was, as always, barking the whole time. Boomer stayed on the other side of the bridge. A game of Stare-Down started between Boomer and Scally. Apparently, the rules for this game were two dogs stared at each other until one of them flinched. Once this happened, it became a matter of running circles around the bridge until one of the participants gave up and headed elsewhere.

Mostly Maggie at Doggy Day Camp

Stare-Down was only a two-player game, and Wags became extremely vocal in his displeasure at not being one of those two. His barking was incessant and disruptive and was an added distraction to the counselors, all of whom were on duty in the playroom to monitor the interaction between the two new dogs and the regulars. Any effort to quiet Wags was completely ignored. He just kept barking. This earned him another spray from the water bottle. Poor Wags had to contend with new campers, Scally playing with other dogs, and also try to please all the counselors present. Poor Wags.

Hotshot arrived. Obviously, there would be no rest for the counselors that morning. Hotshot was a feisty little Chihuahua who sported a diamond stud in one ear. He was perpetual motion, afraid of nothing, and completely oblivious to the fact that he was a very small dog.

The instant he came through the door, he dashed up onto the bridge where I was sitting for a minute, jumped into my lap and was rubbing all over me. I was pleasantly surprised. Hotshot was not usually this friendly with the counselors. Then one of the other counselors told me that what I thought was a rare show of affection, was really just Hotshot trying to rub off some kind of skin ointment. Yuck. So much for affection.

When he'd quite finished rubbing his oily treatment off of himself and onto the entire front of me, he zipped around to greet everybody, including the new ones. Hotshot gave little Shorty a polite sniff and a wag and hurried over to meet big, happy Boomer.

Oh, boy. Hotshot was absolutely thrilled with Boomer, who towered over him. This didn't bother Hotshot at all. He was zipping in and out of Boomer's legs, jumping up in Boomer's face, challenging Boomer to a game of Chase. Boomer thought this was a grand idea, but he was soon left in Hotshot's dust. If Boomer got too close, Hotshot just zoomed under him or under the bridge or under any other taller dog and was out of Boomer's reach. Boomer chased the speedy little guy around for a while, but gave up and headed off to play with someone his own size. Hotshot was not put off by this at all. He continued zipping all around, pestering any dog or counselor he felt like pestering. That was pretty much everybody.

"Oh, who did that? Guess I'd better mop up." Here, I had thought it might be a quiet day.

"Wags. Wags. Wags! Pu-leeeze be quiet." Goodness. His barking was constant. Much as I hated to do it, I resorted to the water bottle myself. He'd gotten it from at least two other counselors already, and it was fairly early in the day. He was beginning to look like he'd stuck his head in the shower, but he did stop barking. At least for the time being. Poor Wags.

Snowball was on her feet, the drinking water the focus of her attention. Snowball dearly loved to tip it over and stretch out in the flood. She did just that. Once Snowball's waterbed had been mopped up and the water dish refilled, Scally immediately ran over to the dish.

All the activity surrounding the drinking dish must have reminded him he was thirsty. Scally stuck his entire muzzle right down to the bottom of the just-filled dish and yanked his head up, creating a great splash in the whole area and practically emptying the dish again. Again, it was mop time and refill time. Done.

"Scally, NO. Not in the drinking water."

Scally also had this thing about relieving himself in the drinking dish. Scally tried his aim at least once every visit. This time we knew we hadn't caught him in time. Whenever he even hesitated for a second at the water dish and he wasn't drinking, it was taken out, scrubbed, sanitized, and refilled yet again, and then brought back into the room. We had no idea what the fascination was for him. He tried this little trick every single time he came to camp. We strongly discouraged him each time, but soon realized this was an exercise in futility. We discouraged him anyway.

Duchess had been watching Scally's behavior with great disdain. Scally apparently found her obvious scorn enticing "You're beautiful when you're angry." So, he approached her. Gentleman-like, but still macho, he slapped his front paws on the floor in front of her in a classic play bow, doing his level best to impress her and get her to play with him. Front legs on the floor, rear end in the air, tail held high, Scally threw his head back and let loose his best and loudest "Ah-rooooo-ooooo-rooo" to gain her favor. Alas, to no avail. Duchess gave him a very quiet and regal growl that immediately put Scally in his place. He gave up. You simply do not mess with the Duchess.

Mostly Maggie at Doggy Day Camp

Scally's attention to Duchess created a little panic in his pal, Wags. This was interesting because Wags played with everybody. He just didn't like it when Scally tried to play with anyone else. Wags set up a terrific din, barking, yowling, and whining at his buddy. He simply would not stop. Time to put the water bottle to work again. Poor Wags.

I decided maybe it was time for me to take a break. There were plenty of counselors in the room. With Wags at his barking best, the noise level had increased by several decibels. With Hotshot and new Boomer there, too, the races were frequent and rowdy. Add Maggie and Scally to the mix and this day was becoming even more hectic than most days. It was turning out to be an incredibly active and fun day, just the kind of day I preferred. Happy dogs to keep me busy.

Coming back into the playroom, I was astonished when Wags dashed right over to me, his furry little head absolutely soaked. He was very friendly, rare for this, my most fractious charge. I was both surprised and delighted at this show of affection, and I lavished him with praise and pets. Then I figured it out.

It was a self-defense thing, a ploy to avoid the water bottle. This dog was just trying to make me feel guilty for squirting him. Of course, I knew he wasn't really trying to make me feel guilty. Nonetheless, it worked. I felt guilty enough to play ball with him again, making sure to keep my fingers and thumbs out of his way this time.

Scally was behaving like a dog on a mission. He was immediately taken into the elimination station, on the off chance he would actually relieve himself in the appropriate area. Wags noticed his friend was no longer in sight and started to carry on something fierce.

"Wags, you'll see Scally in just a minute. Don't carry on so."

We knew this particular racket was only because Scally was out of the room. We knew Wags would be fine once Scally returned, so we spared him yet another spray. Scally returned from his unsuccessful trip and Wags calmed right down. He was back to just his normal level of barking.

Based on the growing number of dogs concentrated around the kitchen door, it was obviously nearing lunch time. Shorty, the new little guy, didn't know exactly why, but he sensed the overall excitement in the room and joined the group now just hanging around watching the kitchen door. Boomer, the new big dog, was really interested in the kitchen.

Scally's presence required the little fence be up in front of the kitchen door to keep him from opening it. The fence was in place, and most everybody steered clear of it. It was a flimsy little fence, but even Scally and Maggie were intimidated by it. Not so, Boomer.

One front Boomer foot went to the top of the half door, the other a little lower down on the fence. His hind feet were hanging onto one of the rods about half-way up the wobbly fence. He was in an undoubtedly precarious position. It couldn't possibly have been a comfortable place for Boomer. Chris and I rushed over to get him off the door and the fence before catastrophe struck. We, quite literally, saved Boomer's butt. It must have been a mighty uncomfortable place. That was the first and last time he got himself in that position.

The dogs started leaving the playroom, headed for the crates. Wags was among the first to be taken out. Normally he and Scally went back together. Not this time. This meant it was Scally's turn to carry on because his friend was no longer in sight. With these two, any separation always created panic.

"Scally, you'll see Wags in just a minute. Don't carry on so."

It was interesting that the dog doing the leaving was not upset while the dog that had been left became anxious. The behavior was the same with either dog. Again, we knew this was temporary, and we tried to reassure him. He carried on something fierce anyway, until he was reunited with Wags inside their crate. These were the only two dogs that shared a crate, a special request by their people.

Boomer went into his crate without hesitation. Once the door was closed, though, he didn't like it one little bit. Our oh-so-happy newcomer spent a big part of naptime making the most pitiful barky-whiny sounds imaginable. He fussed every time he came to camp and that crate door closed behind him. He would finally settle down after about 45 minutes.

It was my opinion that Boomer just didn't want to miss out on anything and crating cramped his style. He was the most lovable, over-the-top clown of a dog

Everybody should have Boomer's joyful view of life.

~ An Unsound Test ~

My granddaughter, Rachael, was working on a junior high science project. We both thought it might be interesting to study the camp dogs in action. Rachael would have recordings of various common sounds a dog would hear over a period of time. A fire siren, a train, a train whistle, a car horn, and several other sounds were included. Rachael would stay out of sight and play the recording. I would be in the playroom monitoring the dogs and reporting individual dog reactions to her. This little adventure could create quite a stir with the dogs. Was I crazy to instigate possible bedlam? I told her this was something that would definitely require prior approval of the camp.

I explained the project to Kate, mentioning that Rachael would like her dog, Bandit, to participate along with all the other dogs. Kate trusted my judgment as to Bandit's health and temperament. When she gave us the go-ahead I thanked her. Maybe Kate was crazy, too?

I called Rachael with the good news, and we picked a day when there would most likely be the highest number of dogs in camp. She immediately began collecting her test sounds and creating a chart for each of a possible dozen dogs that would be in the large playroom. These charts would be labeled with type of dog, a list of all the sounds played. For each sound her charts also included a numbering system from one to ten that would indicate the level of response from each dog. She had allowed space for comments as well. She was very organized and very thorough.

The big day arrived. The test was set for mid-afternoon. I was curious about which dogs would be there to participate in the project. I soon found out.

Snowball came in. I didn't know if that would be good or bad. Given her meltdown experience with the roof workers, I wasn't sure how she would react. These test sounds would be mostly familiar sounds and wouldn't be nearly as loud as the roof noises. Maybe she would take it all in stride. I hoped so.

Then Maggie came in. I wasn't too concerned about her freaking out and she should be just fine. Bonnie and Clyde showed up. In came Cedric and Duchess. I didn't expect any of them to have much of a reaction to much of anything. Well, maybe Clyde would react a little.

Lady came in, and I was sure she would be inquisitive about the sounds. She was followed by Scally and Wags. Now these two could prove interesting. As rambunctious as they both were and as vocal as Wags was, these two might set off a chain reaction if the noises struck them just right. Just wrong?

Boomer was the last to arrive. I expected him to give Rachael the biggest reaction of any of the dogs. He was so curious about everything I figured he'd be running the room perimeter looking for the sounds. Late in the morning in zipped Hotshot. He was another one I thought would react big time.

Bonnie and Clyde were in a corner ignoring everybody. Duchess went to her post at the door. Cedric meandered around the room, stopping long enough to give Snowball a quick greeting. Snowball greeted Lady. Boomer and Maggie were dashing around in a race.

Scally gave a thought to pestering Duchess, but thought better of it. He was still miffed at her spurning his earlier advances. Wags was trying to get in on the race and barking full tilt. Speedy little Hotshot was zooming after all the runners and jumping up in their faces at every opportunity. A pretty good group on a pretty normal day. I was confident this would be a great group for Rachael's science project sound test.

Noon arrived and we crated up, fed, and watered our furry charges. They all settled down for the two-hour rest time. After standard room cleaning and other nap time chores, I headed home to check on Toby. My daughter, Jenni, Rachael, and my grandson, Anthony, were due to arrive at camp at three o'clock or so. I had plenty of time to get back over there for the big test.

Mostly Maggie at Doggy Day Camp

I headed back to work, arriving about ten minutes before my family showed up. I was happy to see the morning dogs were still at camp, and as a bonus, Hot Shot had come in. We set up it all. There were no dogs in the smaller room. Rachael, Jenni, and Anthony would play the recordings from there, out of sight and silent. They were hiding just inside the Dutch door separating the rooms, the top half of that door open. Kate was with them. If Rachael needed to say anything, Kate's voice was familiar to the dogs and would not cause an unwanted distraction.

Three other counselors had graciously volunteered to help and were in with the dogs and me. We had all been assigned specific dogs to watch. It wouldn't hurt to have extra hands available in case any of the sounds caused a big commotion. Counselors would identify the dog and his reaction and Rachael would record it. Boy, we were ready.

I brought Bandit into the room. The one thing that had never occurred to anybody was that Bandit might not be comfortable with the camp dogs. She was a real sociable dog, and we all thought she'd be happy to race around. Naturally all the campers zipped over to welcome the newcomer. Bandit hated it from the get-go. Hoping she would get over the doggy introductions and join in, I tried to get her away from me and interested in playing. It didn't work. As soon as she had an opportunity, she split away from the regulars and stuck herself to my leg, quite determined to stay there for the duration. The campers decided she wasn't worth any more of their time and went off to do other things.

Rachael and her assistants might have been totally out of sight, but Bandit knew exactly where they were and sort of nudged me in the direction of the small room. Because she was so nervous, I went along with her, figuring I could relay information on the other dogs just as well from that point. She quietly whined, wanting to rejoin her people. She eventually did settle down but would not have anything to do with the campers. That was a disappointment.

The sound tape started rolling. Reactions from the dogs? There weren't any. At least not enough to be of any value. The taped sounds were not loud enough. They were barely audible, in fact. I knew my hearing wasn't what it should be, but I certainly should have heard something. I asked the other counselors, and they also had trouble hearing the tapes. Those sounds that they could hear were extremely quiet.

The dogs, even with their hearing capabilities, didn't take much notice at all. It was true they were all busy with normal dog games, but the recordings were exceptionally quiet and would have been too quiet even if the dogs had been sleeping.

At the sound of the fire siren, Boomer tilted his head a fraction. Maggie stood still for about a second at the marching band music, but almost immediately went back to racing with Boomer. Hotshot was totally absorbed in pestering everybody he could and ignored any sounds at all. Duchess was too intrigued with watching the bottom of the door. From his vantage point on top of the bridge, Cedric was only interested in spotting Kate. Bonnie and Clyde were concentrating strictly on each other. Lady was looking for pets from the counselors. Scally was trying to decide if counselors would notice he was about to add water of his own to the drinking dish. Wags was barking his way around the room. Good ol' Snowball was snoozing in her corner. Bandit was so intent on getting to her people beyond that door we could have fired off a cannon and she would have ignored it.

Overall, I would have to say the big junior high science project wound up as a bust. The sounds had been so faint they were virtually ignored. At that point there was nothing we could do to improve things. We couldn't up the volume.

Rachael was understandably disappointed. The whole camp crew, as well as her mom and I, had been sure the project would be a success. When it wasn't, we all sympathized with her. Geez, it had been such a flop that even Anthony, her little brother, felt bad for her.

Rachael gathered up test gear and Bandit. She thanked Kate and crew for allowing her to give it a try. On a bit of a sad and unsuccessful note, my family and I left camp. On a much happier note, Bandit gladly left with us.

Oh, well. The best-laid plans...

~ Where There's No Smoke. . . ~

There was no doubt it was going to be a busy, busy morning. We already had eight dogs scheduled for camp. These included Maggie, Boomer, Hotshot, and Sassy, four of the most active of the day campers. I was also expecting Snowball, Duchess, Cedric, and Lady. This was a good bunch, especially on that day.

There would a visitor from Corporate Headquarters as well. When a company official came, it was always good to have a fair to large number of dogs in the playroom. It was a good way to impress the big bosses. It was too bad the smaller room was not in use. That would have impressed Corporate even more. Oh, well. It was still an impressive group.

Maggie was the first to arrive as usual. Snowball and Sassy came in right behind her and the three of them wasted no time getting down to some serious playing. Duchess and Cedric entered and headed to their normal positions. Duchess took guard duty at the bottom of the door and Cedric on top of the bridge. Lady came and joined Maggie and Sassy in a chase around the room.

In came Annie, a Chocolate Lab. Annie was an avid ball player and would chase a thrown ball as many times as someone would throw it. I didn't have to worry about puncture wounds when I played ball with Annie. She always stuck to the rules. She also played pretty well with the other dogs. She was very affectionate and well-behaved.

Tawny, a Golden Retriever and Annie's housemate, came in with her. Tawny loved everybody. Once inside the playroom, she ran around to greet all her buddies. Tawny loved to play, loved to jump up on the bridge, and jump right back down again. Greetings out of the way, she was up on the bridge, down off the bridge, up on the bridge, down off the bridge. She was obviously happy to be at camp.

Oh-oh. First clean-up of the day.

In came Boomer. He zipped over to greet me, ran over to Maggie, zoomed across to Sassy, and dashed over to Duchess, moving so fast that Duchess didn't even have time to give him a grumpy growl. He galloped over to Annie, got right in Cedric's face, rushed over to Lady, and checked in with Tawny. Tawny jumped up on the bridge, displacing Cedric, who trotted over to Duchess. Boomer jumped up on the bridge, displacing Tawny. Then he jumped off the bridge, giving my arm a sloppy slurp in greeting as he raced past.

All the dogs were extremely busy, and Maggie was the first to notice that Spike Weimaraner had arrived. She greeted him before anyone else even knew he was there. Spike W. was always full of energy. The rest of the big dogs spotted him, and he got a group welcome. There were dogs running all over the room.

What a fun bunch this was. Our Corporate visitor would be happy to see all these dogs and all the activity. Even when we weren't expecting visitors, I liked it when we were as busy as we were that day. There was never a dull moment on days like that. Then, this day turned out to be a wild one. It was about get even wilder. Hotshot came zipping in.

Hotshot truly had no concept of size. He ran after Maggie, jumping up at her and barking in her face. Then he zipped away and went zigging and zagging in and out under the bridge. Sassy tried to follow him, but couldn't keep up. Hotshot charged Boomer and Lady and Annie and Tawny. He feared nothing. Not one of the big dogs could keep up with him. He was so quick and so small, he could get anywhere faster than anyone else. He absolutely could not be still for a minute.

Things were moving right along. All the dogs were active and were getting along well. It was a good time for me to head out for my break. As I walked through the store, I got a whiff of a peculiar odor that hadn't been noticeable in the camp area. I didn't give it much thought.

After my break I headed back. At the door to the camp area, I met a customer with a dog to be groomed and a baby in a stroller. I volunteered to hold her dog and the door. We were about half way through the entry when Kate came up behind us. She very calmly and very quietly informed the customer and me that we were evacuating the building. There seemed to be a fire somewhere in the store. That explained the smell. The customer wheeled the stroller around, took her dog, and left the building. Customers were quickly and quietly being evacuated.

Kate and I hustled into the playroom and informed the counselors the fire department was on its way. There was no smoke visible. We couldn't see any flames, but the smell was stronger now and definitely identifiable as something burning. It had reached the playrooms and was getting stronger by the minute. We had to get all the dogs, eleven from day camp and three from grooming, out of the building, and we had to do it calmly. There was no panic.

It was quickly decided that the best route would not be through the emergency door in the smaller room that Snowball had tested for us early on. "Why not?" you might ask and rightfully so. There were a couple of reasons it made more sense for us to take the dogs out the front doors, a slightly longer path to safety.

While we did have to evacuate the dogs quickly, there were no flames and there was no smoke. We were moving the dogs out based on a smell only. The dogs had sensed something was going on and had gathered together in anticipation of they-didn't-know-what so they were already a little excited. Taking them out by a route that was familiar to all of them would cause the least amount of confusion. Those staff members not assigned to evacuating customers had also gathered in the camp lobby so dogs and people were in one area.

We counselors put leads on all the dogs and handed them off to whoever was available. Camp counselors, groomers, and floor employees all pitched in. There was no discussion about who would take which dog. You took the one, in some cases two, handed to you and led him through the store and out to the front parking lot.

I had two dogs on leads—Annie, the quiet Chocolate Lab, and the always lively Boomer. The General Manager came in and was ready to take a dog. For a split second, I actually thought about handing wild and crazy Boomer over to him. Before that thought was even fully formulated in my head, I came to my senses. That just wouldn't be right. The manager was not at all familiar with wild and crazy Boomer. I was. I gave him quiet Annie, and I kept Boomer, who gave one quick tug on his lead. This got him an immediate reprimand, and he calmed down instantly. We headed out. Boomer behaved extremely well all the way.

All of us cleared the building in organized short order. No panic. No confusion. No problems whatsoever. While these dogs were well behaved, they were all pretty rambunctious under normal circumstances. On this day they were all calm and obedient. They exceeded everyone's expectations under highly unusual circumstances. Every single one of them was fully cooperating. Must have been The Tone.

You would most likely recognize The Tone. It's the one adults, mostly moms, use in emergencies, the voice that is never questioned, the voice that says, "This is serious, don't give me any flack, just give me immediate response." All of that is conveyed solely through The Tone Words beyond a spoken name are totally unnecessary to get instant attention and that attention stays focused until further instructions are given. It's not something that can be pulled up at will. If there is not a true emergency in progress, The Tone simply doesn't exist. A possible fire in the building qualified as a true emergency. It quickly became obvious that The Tone has the same effect on dogs as it does on children.

We ended up on a grassy island in the parking lot. Kate, our manager, was always cheerful, calm, and efficient. She made the best of any situation. She was a gem. This particular morning was no different. Kate announced that we were on a field trip. She made everyone laugh and effectively got rid of any tension in both dogs and people. So we took advantage of being outside on our field trip in the sunshine for however long we would be out there.

The fire trucks arrived almost immediately and the firemen went inside. Counselors, groomers, and floor staff were all out in front of the store, waiting to find out if we would be going back inside or if we would be out of work soon. We all wondered, too, if the evacuation plan for all the other animals in the store would have to be implemented. This decision would have to come from Corporate.

The fire couldn't have been too bad because the firemen allowed our General Manager and the visiting Corporate lady to go back inside almost immediately. That was good to hear. It meant the small animals, birds, and fish still inside the store were not in any danger. Word filtered down that we would be going back inside soon.

Mostly Maggie at Doggy Day Camp

A prospective customer pulled into the parking lot. He spotted the fire trucks and the group of dogs and people standing outside. He pulled over and stopped next to our furry group, rolled down his window.

"Hey," he hollered. "What are you selling, hot dogs?" He laughed like crazy at his own joke as he drove off. That made everybody chuckle.

After forty-five minutes or so under the trees, we were allowed back inside. There had been a bit of a smolder going on in the overhead wiring but everything had been handled. The fire department left, and we all went back inside, high-fiving along the way.

When we got everybody back into the playroom, it was right back to normal doggy bedlam. I took a minute to sit on the bridge with Tawny. Boomer zoomed up behind me, gave my ear a mighty slurp, and zoomed back down without dislodging either Tawny or me. Maggie came over and got a water bottle drink. Lady got a requested pet, Spike Weimaraner was running rampant, Sassy was trying to hide behind my knees again, Annie was after a ball, and both Duchess and Cedric were now studying the door. Hotshot was everywhere, and Snowball was sprawled out in her favorite lounge spot.

Yep, it was back to normal.

Corporate had to have been impressed with all of us, dogs and staff alike.

~ Small Room Happenings ~

Polly, a Basset Hound, came into the smaller playroom. She was a very curious older dog and checked out the entire room with her Basset nose and her distinct Basset gait. She loved attention from the counselors, and we always obliged her. Polly wasn't tremendously playful but she did get along well with other quiet dogs. Cedric and Duchess, given their choice of rooms that morning, had elected to join Polly and me. Bonnie and Clyde rounded out our quiet little pack.

Duchess was doing her normal bottom-of-any-door sentinel duty. Cedric was surveying all he could see from the top level of the playhouse. From his perch in this room it was almost impossible for him to spot Kate as she went about the business of managing pet services. Cedric didn't seem to realize that. He kept a watchful eye anyhow. Bonnie and Clyde were wrestling around a little with each other, and Polly was watching from her spot along the wall.

It was extremely difficult to get this group excited about much of anything. I did manage to interest Duchess in her squeaky shoe for just a couple of minutes. I bounced a ball for Cedric who wanted no part of that. Polly, though, chased the ball once or twice. It was normally quiet in the small room, and this morning was no exception. Well, that was about to change.

Hotshot, our dynamo of a Chihuahua, had arrived. He loved absolutely everybody, big or small. I wondered what would happen if he came in with our little crew. In he came. As usual, Hotshot was zipping lickety-split all over the room and in and out of the playhouse. All this activity underneath him in the playhouse actually roused Cedric from his top floor post and he went to the lower level of the house to find out who or what was causing all that commotion. Then the most amazing thing happened.

Hotshot, in his own inimitable manner, somehow convinced Cedric to chase him in and out of that playhouse. Much to my delighted amazement, Hotshot managed to get every single one of my little charges involved in something. He had Polly running around on her stubby little legs. He got Bonnie involved in a race. He managed to get jealous Clyde to race around the room with him and forget about Bonnie for a short time. Most surprising of all, he even had Duchess, our dowager queen, running and playing. It was a wonderful sight to behold. Hotshot never ran out of gas.

When the dogs had had enough excitement, all of about ten minute's worth, they all went back to their normal, sedate routines. Hotshot, of course, was still loaded for bear and looking for action. It wouldn't have been right to keep him in with this now worn-out little group. I thanked Hotshot for his successful efforts and sent him into the big playroom where he could continue to expend his always-frenetic energy. I escorted him into the larger room so he would not be bored.

* * * *

There was the one embarrassing morning in the small room. So far, Queenie and I were the only ones in the small room that day. This was early on and Queenie was still pretty nervous about being at camp and still didn't want much to do with anyone, including me.

There was a furnace problem and Queenie and I were both freezing. I tried to convince her to climb onto my lap for warmth, but she wasn't anxious to do that. I put one of the warm and fuzzy little crate mats on the floor, sat down next to it and stayed very still and quiet. Queenie finally decided that the mat looked like a more comfy place to be, even if it was close to the scary ol' counselor. She cautiously made her way over and sat down next to me. I said nothing for a few minutes. Then I talked softy to her. After a few more minutes, she allowed me to pick her up. I tucked her under my jacket and the two of us hunkered down trying to keep warm. She was content to stay there.

We finally got some heat. I was pleasantly surprised when Queenie stayed on my lap. Before long we were joined by Polly, Bonnie, and Clyde. Queenie left my lap to avoid close contact with the new arrivals that came over to tell us both hello. and to create a puddle, which greatly interested Clyde.

"Oh, yuck, Clyde. Don't slurp that." Time for a quick clean-up.

There was a man working in the corner of the room. One of portable fences had been set up to keep the dogs from helping the guy. All the dogs except Queenie kept putting their little paws up on the fence, and I kept telling them to get down. I decided they needed a distraction.

Me being me, my first inclination was to talk to them. I'm still good at that. I explained the man really didn't need their help. I chattered away at them, thanking them for doing good things. I carried on entire one-sided conversations with them about what was happening in their furry little lives.

I had totally forgotten there was another human being in the room with me. When it dawned on me he was there, I got all flustered and embarrassed. Don't ask me why. I was, after all, the one who had story time for the dogs. In that case, though, nobody but fellow workers could hear me, and they already knew I was a little nuts. However, this guy was not someone I knew. He laughed and told me he was getting a kick out of the whole scenario. Good man

* * * *

One would think that crating the little dogs would be a pretty easy task. It wasn't easy even though most of them were cooperative. They were put on leads, taken to the elimination station just in case, and then lifted into their second level crates. No problems.

Queenie, on the other hand, absolutely hated to be put into her crate. Come lunch/nap time, this usually inactive and shy dog would develop an entirely new personality. She would go into her catch-me-if-you-can mode. She became very quick on her paws and quite adept at avoiding capture. If the counselor was very patient, very calm, and very sneaky, Queenie could eventually be conned into coming close enough to be caught. Counselors had to be sure the crate was ready for Queenie before putting her inside. Once you had her, she settled down and resigned herself to temporary incarceration.

She might have resigned herself, but she didn't like it. The whole while she was inside her crate, her goal was to get out as soon as an opportunity presented itself. You didn't want to open that door again until it was time for her to come out. The instant that crate door opened, Queenie was primed to rocket out at you. Not a good idea, since her crate was on the second level, a long way down for a little dog. Counselors would open the door only wide enough to get an arm in and get hold of Queenie so she could be safely lifted out. We had to be on double alert with quiet little Queenie.

* * * *

I had always considered myself a big dog person. Working with the little ones that came to camp gave me a whole new perspective. I decided I would never again reject a dog based solely on size. I discovered the little ones are just as lovable as the big ones. They aren't all ankle nippers and constant yappers. I should have realized this much sooner in my life.

Most days in the small room were quiet and relaxing. Those few occasions when things got a little exciting just made it more interesting.

Never underestimate the size of a small dog's heart.

~ Sucker for a Shelter Dog ~

    Daylight hadn't yet arrived as I sat in my car in the dark, virtually empty parking lot. I was not in any of the closest fifteen parking places as I waited for the manager to arrive and unlock the building. I hadn't been there long when she pulled into her spot in the side lot, much closer to the building. I got out of my car and started walking toward the door.

    I always try to be aware of what is happening around me, but I hadn't noticed a black pick-up parked four lanes over about halfway between my car and the building. I did notice it when I was almost even with it. I picked up my pace a little. It was dark, the manager had disappeared inside, and there was no one else around. I'd just taken another step when a male voice I didn't recognize called me by name. Well, that was a surprise. Not quite sure what was going on, I slowed down just a little and looked in his direction. I didn't have any idea who he was.

    Just then, two dogs that had been walking at his side came out in front of him. Well, I didn't know him, but I sure knew the two dogs. They were camp regulars. One was Tawny and the other was Annie. Relieved to see familiar faces, I stopped and waited for them.

    The man said he was sorry and hadn't meant to startle me. He introduced himself as the dad of the two dogs. It was normally their mom who brought them in, but she wasn't able to do it that day. He said he knew he was kind of early, but asked if I could please take the dogs from him in the parking lot since he was already running a little late for work. I was happy to oblige him. I had plenty of time to get them settled and do my rounds.

Mostly Maggie at Doggy Day Camp

It was play time. I brought Annie and Tawny into the big room. Snowball, Cedric, Duchess, and deaf Norton soon joined us. Lady came in, followed by Sassy. This was a nice little group with which to work.

Almost an hour into play time, Kate brought a new dog into the big room. He obviously had some Labrador Retriever in his blood, mixed with something unidentified but large. His was not the coat of a Lab but it was not a long coat either. He was big. He was dirty and pretty darned stinky. He had been abandoned. He was very quiet with an almost sad look. Kate called him Bear.

Of course the other dogs gathered around him, checking him out and wagging at him. Bear wasn't exactly thrilled with all their attention, but he tolerated it.

Kate explained he was from a local shelter group and had come in for much-needed grooming. No doubt about it, Bear definitely needed a thorough grooming. He had handsome features and a black coat that could only improve once he was clean. Kate thought he would also benefit from some socializing with the campers. I agreed. She left Bear with me and went off to other duties.

After the ritual new-dog greeting, the campers went off to their own activities. Bear attached himself to me and wasn't anxious to play with the dogs. I wondered about his full background. When I gave him a bit of encouragement, he finally spent a few minutes with Annie, Lady, and Snowball, three other quiet and calm dogs. Sassy and Tawny intimidated him while both Cedric and Duchess ignored him. Little deaf Norton decided to howl.

This sent Bear back to lean on me. I was sitting on the bridge trying to convince Norton everything was good with the world and he could stop howling, which he did eventually. Poor Bear didn't know what to make of Norton howling. Poor Bear didn't quite know what to make of the whole camp thing. He spent the rest of the morning glued to my leg and getting as much petting and individual attention as I could give him. That was a lot. I was unwisely and knowingly letting this hulk of a dirty, stinky, rescued dog get to me.

Bear was a mighty sweet dog, and he had certainly wrapped me around his paw. At lunch time, I mentioned to Kate how sad Bear looked and that I hoped he would find a good home. Big mistake.

After morning janitorial duties, I told Bear good-bye as he headed for his much-needed grooming. I headed home where Toby waited. It was about mid-afternoon when my phone rang. Caller ID told me it was work. I should have ignored it. I didn't.

"Woof, woof, woof. Bow-wow-wow."

That was what I heard when I answered. Knowing I don't always hear well, I asked the caller to repeat what they'd said.

"Woof, woof, woof. Bow-wow-wow."

Okay, same thing. Then it hit me, and I burst out laughing. It was Kate. She had called to convince me in dog-speak to come and pick up a freshly cleaned-up Bear and give him a forever home. I declined, giving her all the reasons why we didn't need a second dog. Toby would feel bad having to share Tom and me, Bear was a really big dog, Tom would never agree. etc. etc. She wasn't buying any of it. I told her I'd think about it.

I thought about it for all of about two minutes. Bear really was a nice dog. I ended up calling Tom at work, asking him about the possibility of adding Bear to our family. He said he didn't think it was a good idea. I kind of whimpered at him, and he agreed to get home as soon as possible and go over to the store and at least meet Bear.

As soon as he pulled in the driveway, I dashed out to the car. We didn't have much time. The camp would close in half an hour. He drove like the wind, and we got there in record time. I jumped out of the car, raced into the store, and back to camp.

Kate was waiting for us. So was Bear. He looked fabulous, his black coat shining and soft. His aroma was distinctly better than it had been in the morning. I couldn't believe it was the same dog.

It seems his session with the groomer, combined with a day in the playroom with a bunch of other dogs had perked him right up. He didn't look sad any more. He wasn't clinging to a person any more. He had, in fact, become a totally rowdy, completely unruly and boisterous dog. He was normal.

By then, I really couldn't believe it was the same dog. What in the world had happened to that calm, affectionate dog that had spent the morning oh-so-quietly working his way into my heart? He was still a fine dog, and a good-looking one.

Mostly Maggie at Doggy Day Camp

The quiet dog I'd spent time with that very morning had disappeared completely. His shyness was one of the reasons I'd even considered adopting him. That dog would have been an excellent companion for Toby. This new and improved version would have driven poor Toby crazy. It turned out that he just would not be a good match for our family—not for Tom, not for me, and definitely not for Toby.

None of us would have been able to keep up with him. Bear would have been bored to doggy tears in our house. He needed a home with a lot of active kids. Tom and I both felt bad, but we simply couldn't take him. It wouldn't have been fair to Toby, and it wouldn't have been fair to Bear. With all his good points, and he did have many, I was confident he would find a happy, commotion-filled home. He would love that.

It wasn't an easy decision but we left camp without Bear.

I knew better. This showed precisely why I could never work at a shelter.

~ A Scary Situation ~

One morning, the dogs that came in were all regulars and were well-known to all of the counselors. This was an active and fun bunch, sometimes rowdy, but never any problem. I was alone with the dogs today. Everybody else was busy in other parts of the building. This had never happened before. There was no one in the camp lobby, no one in the grooming area, no one in sight of the playroom. Oh, I'd been alone in the playroom many times, as had other counselors, but this was the first time any counselor had been virtually isolated with the dogs. I was not concerned. I knew each of these dogs very well.

They were all big dogs: Maggie, the Great Dane; Diablo, the Shepherd mix; Spike, the Weimaraner; Boomer, the German Shorthair mix; Lady, another German Shorthair mix; and Casper, another Shepherd mix.

It was about mid-morning and the dogs were all very busy, playing in groups of two or three. This was normal behavior. After a few minutes, things got interesting.

It was incredibly rare for all of the dogs, on any day, to be playing one game together, but they were doing it now. They were all racing round and round the room as a loose pack, having a good ol' time for several minutes. Suddenly something else started happening. I couldn't put my finger on exactly what it was, but the atmosphere had changed. I could feel it.

Instead of the whole group just racing around, five of the six dogs now seemed to have become an organized pack. That pack had targeted Maggie for some reason or other. She'd been racing with them, but they seemed now to be actually chasing her. They were all barking and poking at her, and she was becoming a little bit nervous. I had no idea what the goal of the five was, but I didn't like this at all. Maggie liked it even less, and that could easily turn quickly into a disaster.

I couldn't tell you the precise moment the race turned into the chase, but I knew I had to stop it, and I had to stop it instantly. I got on the walkie-talkie and requested immediate help. I really couldn't wait for back-up to arrive, though. I was on my own here, and it was not a comfortable feeling. I wasn't afraid, but I was a little apprehensive. I absolutely had to do something immediately.

I had the can of Citronella for use in extreme emergencies. I didn't want to use it. It was getting pretty close, but we were not to the critical point just yet. I didn't want to let the situation reach that critical point. So far, it was only to the this-is-obviously-not-good point, requiring prompt action, but not extreme enough for the Citronella spray.

While nobody appeared to be seriously aggressive yet, I really feared for Maggie—both what they might do to her and what she might do to them if she got any more upset than she was at that moment. Nothing for it but to wade through the pack and physically break them up.

I started calling dogs by name, spraying the water bottle at everybody, trying to slow them all down, and get them away from Maggie. They did slow down a bit, but they were still in a tight bunch and still barking at her. Large as she was, Maggie was, after all, still a puppy. It was obvious she was a becoming more than a little upset with being surrounded with no safe haven in sight. She was trapped against the wall.

I pushed dogs aside right and left with no threats from the pack and was able to get close enough to Maggie to calm her down a bit. When the other dogs were forced away from her, I managed to get a lead around her neck. For her own safety, and to re-direct the rest of the dogs, I figured my best option at that point was to place Maggie in protective custody and take her out of the room.

By the time I got the other dogs away from her and pulled her out of the fray, the feeling of impending doom had gone down by several degrees and help had arrived. The other counselors had certainly not been slow to respond. They got back to the camp area almost immediately. The situation in the playroom had just happened incredibly fast.

Maggie was taken out of the room and put in the kennel area until she could calm down. The rest of the dogs needed to calm down as well. So did I.

The pack had broken up and the dogs were back to playing in smaller groups. Maggie had been out for about twenty minutes. We decided to bring her back now that we had three counselors in the playroom. The three of us kept a very close and wary eye on everybody.

It was like nothing had ever happened. The dogs had forgotten the whole thing, even Maggie. She was busy running with Diablo. Lady and Boomer were chasing the ball. Spike and Casper were playing Tuggie. Things ran smoothly for the rest of the morning.

The crisis, if it really was a crisis, was over. Could it have been my imagination? No. I didn't think so at the time, and I don't think so today. Something decidedly unpleasant had been going on.

I wasn't afraid for my own safety with these dogs, even when they were acting as a pack. I admit, though, that the sudden and completely unexpected mob mentality I saw in my charges that day set my nerves on edge. I was more than a little relieved when reinforcements arrived.

We had been told back during our training that Corporate felt only one counselor was needed for every twenty dogs. Someone had disagreed and argued that one was not enough. It would be difficult for a single counselor to monitor that many dogs because dogs, being dogs, could get out of hand. Luckily, Corporate had listened to reason.

Twenty to one odds in favor of the dogs was flat-out just plain risky. It was never more evident than on this day when I was dealing with only six dogs.

The walkie-talkies were seldom used. Most of the time, when we used them it was to call another counselor into the playroom so whoever was already in there could take a break. That day, however, the walkie-talkies had been invaluable and had definitely served their intended function. I was glad we had them.

This particular incident was so unusual that it will stand out in my mind for a long, long time as being just a little bit scary. That was the last time any counselor was left in such a truly isolated situation.

I was also more than thankful I had not had to resort to the Citronella spray.

Dogs never hold a grudge, an attribute we should all take to heart.

~ Another Day - Another Collar ~

It was another day with not a lot of dogs scheduled, but that didn't mean much. We usually got a drop-in or two, or three, or four.

Jake came in. He was a Shepherd/Husky mix who was far and away the most handsome dog I'd ever seen. His back stood about hip-high and he was absolutely gorgeous. He had a Shepherd face, ears, and long, slender legs. His coat felt like that of a Shepherd, but it looked like spun gold. His nose was black, but everything else was warm yellow-gold, including his eyes. He had it all. The look of a golden canine Adonis and a sweet disposition to boot. He was a great dog and got along well with everybody. When Jake wanted your attention he would push his head into you, front or back, at just the right level to make you jump. He would run with the big guys, and would play Tuggie with a little Dachshund named Dolly.

Dolly came in shortly after Jake. She was slightly overweight even though she was a fairly active little gal. She would occasionally race around with Jake on her pudgy little legs. She starting running with him. Jake located the tug toy and the two of them had a go at that. It was really funny to watch those two play anything with each other.

Dolly's all-time favorite game, though, consisted of only two players; Dolly and a counselor, me this time. She had a favorite ball that she would push in my direction. She never grabbed for it and actually waited patiently for me to roll it again. I didn't throw a ball for Dolly. She only chased rolling balls. She always chased it when I rolled it, and she always brought it back to me, sort of. She would stop about four feet in front of me, drop her ball and push it at me with her nose.

Mostly Maggie at Doggy Day Camp

Spike, a huge Rottweiler, came into the room. He was another of those dogs who never kicked up a fuss and was always quiet and calm. He was an older dog and spent most of his time napping. He didn't play with anybody, but he liked to have his head rubbed now and then. Spike Rottweiler picked a spot along the playroom wall and pretty much stayed put.

Pixie, a Yorkie with a punk hair style, came that day. Her hair was clipped short and stuck out just every which way. She was the tiniest dog I had ever seen. Pixie would fit in one hand and was one hundred percent adorable. She went immediately over to Dolly and ran on over to greet Jake. Another case of size meaning nothing. There wasn't a bone of fear in this tiny dog. No wallflower, Pixie. She would zip all over the playroom without ever getting stepped on by the big guys. That always amazed me.

Snowball loped into camp. She greeted the others, ran with Jake for a few minutes, and then headed for her favorite lounge spot in the corner. Pixie went over to her and cuddled up at her side, a tiny bundle of black and brown and tan against a mountain of white. Geez, I should have had a camera with me at all times.

In came Hotshot. He zipped in and greeted Jake, Dolly, and Spike. He'd never met Pixie before. When he noticed her, he dashed right over for a how-do-you-do? While Hotshot paid no mind to the size of any of the dogs, I couldn't help but wonder if he realized that, on this day, he was not the smallest dog in attendance. Pixie and Hotshot checked each other out thoroughly and wrestled around a little. It was great. They each finally had someone they could actually wrestle with for a change. They could run with the big dogs for a little while, but they sure couldn't wrestle with them.

In came our other Spike, the wound-up Weimaraner. He ran over to Spike Rottweiler, who just wanted to be left alone. Spike W. didn't take offense and immediately ran over to Jake to invite him to race. Dolly was abandoned. Jake and Spike W. tore off running around the room, Spike W. barking along the way.

Hotshot and Pixie were involved in a race of their own. It was comical when both of these tiny dogs decided to join Jake and Spike Weimaraner. This didn't last long, and the little ones went back to their own race, staying out of the way of the thundering Jake and Spike W. They weren't afraid of the big dogs, but they were both smart enough to keep out from underfoot when there was a big-dog race in progress.

Along about mid-morning, we were graced with the presence of Jeeves. I dearly loved Jeeves, an older Golden Retriever who was almost as mellow as Snowball. He played with everybody. Evidently this hadn't always been the case. His people told us he had gone through a socialization class because he had been extremely aggressive toward other dogs. That class had obviously worked. Jeeves would most certainly win a Mr. Congeniality contest.

It was hard to believe this gentle old dog had ever had aggression problems. Made me think every dog, aggressive or not, should take such a class at the earliest possible age. Anyway, he kind of sauntered around the room greeting everybody. He was gentle, most affectionate, loved to please, and was really cooperative in the playroom. He was just a sweetheart of a dog.

Spike Weimaraner and Jake were still running all over the place and Jeeves joined them. He circled the room with them a time or two and then went into his own thing. His own thing consisted of running at top speed toward a wall, turning just before his face smashed into it, and throwing his entire body against the wall. This made a terrible racket and we counselors worried he would hurt himself. Thank goodness, he only did it once in a while, and he never seemed the worse for wear. We didn't know why he did this, but he certainly seemed to enjoy it. Was he taking out his former aggression on a wall rather than on another dog? We had no idea.

Having two dogs with the same name in the same room at the same time was always interesting. In this case, we occasionally had to correct the rowdy Spike Weimaraner, so we would call his name and get on his case a little. Meantime, the oh-so-sweet Spike Rottweiler was still in his prone position, not bothering anybody. His head came up, and he looked at us with a what? look on his face. He got a pet and was assured he was not in any trouble. His head went right back down on his paws. Spike Weimaraner, on the other hand, assumed we must not be talking to him and continued his nonsense barking until he got a spritz from the water bottle.

Mostly Maggie at Doggy Day Camp

Lunch time was rapidly approaching, and the dogs took up their kitchen-watch stations. It was time to put them back into their crates. Spike R. moseyed on back and got right into his crate. Rowdy as he was, Spike Weimaraner went into his crate with no trouble. Jeeves, on the other hand, was the champion of attempted crate avoidance. I'm not kidding. Jeeves would have been a gold medal winner in this category, if they had one.

Jeeves must have practiced his sad face in a mirror. He looked heartbroken. Come crate time, Jeeves was absolutely pathetic. This was Jeeves the gentle, Jeeves the affectionate, Jeeves who actually obeyed when given a command, yes, Jeeves the always cooperative, Jeeves the happy except at crate time. He was still gentle. He was still affectionate. He still listened. Come crate time, however, Jeeves was definitely not cooperative. He was definitely not happy. In fact, Jeeves developed a serious case of the stubborns at crate time.

He would sit himself down, leaning as hard as he could on the crates behind him. Jeeves looked at me with his whole expressive face.

"I'm really, really, really sorry. I know my sitting here instead of going into that stupid crate is disappointing to you. I really don't like to disappoint you. Really, I don't. The thing of it is, you know, that I hate going in there, and I am just not going to do it. Please don't be mad at me, and please don't make me go inside that thing. I'll be fine out here. Honest. Cross my heart. I won't cause any problems. I'll be good as gold, you'll see. I really, really don't want to go inside that dumb crate. Aw, geez, I'll be good right here. Pulee-e-e-z-e don't make me go in there."

Jeeves had not only an expressive face. He also had quite a large vocabulary, as you can see.

I gave him a tug. I gave him a hug. I reassured him. I coaxed him. I cajoled him. Eventually his guilt always got the better of him and he sulked his way into the crate. Jeeves never ever went into a crate willingly and I don't believe he ever will. I dearly loved Jeeves.

You just have to love a good dog even when he's being incredibly stubborn.

~ More Stuff Happens ~

Sometimes things just occur, over which you have no real control. Much as you think the day will be full of normal doggy behavior, you cannot escape the sneak-up-on-you events. It could be something funny. It might be something not so funny. It might be something so far out that it leaves you scratching your head.

* * * *

One morning, a store employee brought her cat in to work to be groomed. The cat lived with one of the dogs who was in camp that day. She carried the cat over to the Dutch door. She had unescorted access to this door because she was an employee. She was about to open that door and take her cat on in. I was dumbfounded. I told her she absolutely could not go into the playroom with a cat. She calmly informed me that it would be okay because her cat liked dogs. She did not enter the playroom.

Instead, she held the cat up over the half door, in full view of the seven or eight dogs in the playroom. This, of course, was an invitation to all of the dogs to gather 'round and inspect this unfamiliar critter. I insisted that she immediately take the cat out of the camp area and out of sight of the dogs. She repeated that her cat liked dogs.

"Well, maybe not all these dogs like cats," I pointed out. She hadn't thought of that.

Now cats run pretty much neck and neck with dogs as far as me liking them, but even to think about entering a room full of strange dogs with a cat just made no sense to me.

She and her cat reluctantly left the camp area. I assume I'd made my point. Thereafter that cat came in only for grooming and never again got close to the dogs.

* * * *

One afternoon we had a very young dog, Riley, in camp. Riley was a feisty Golden Retriever, about seven months old. She was one who really loved to be around people.

It was getting late and all the other dogs had been picked up. We figured we could start cleaning up as we often did when there was only one dog left. That one dog would follow the counselors around, helping with the chores. I was working in the kitchen, and Chris was vacuuming the playroom. Riley was under the bridge staying out of the way, and we thought that was great.

When her mom came to pick her up, though, Riley stayed under the bridge. She was at the far end of the big playroom. Riley was just watching. This was an unexpected reaction from a dog who usually couldn't greet her people soon enough.

As soon as the vacuum was turned off, she rocketed out from under the bridge and literally threw herself at her mom. As it turned out, Riley was actually hiding under the bridge. During the first camp interview the fact that Riley was afraid of vacuum cleaners had never come up. Why would it? I'm sure the owners didn't anticipate vacuuming at camp. Poor Riley.

While the other dogs liked to help, little Riley had been terrified of the vacuum, and we hadn't realized it. From then on, we made sure any last dog was not unnerved by our chores.

* * * *

Then there was the problem we didn't even know about for at least a couple of weeks after the fact. We received a reprimand from Corporate, located out of state, because a store customer had complained.

Evidently, she'd been watching the dogs in the playroom, and they looked bored, especially the big white one. She said that a counselor was sitting on the bridge reading and not paying any attention to the dogs. We all wished she had mentioned it at the time.

We didn't know who the customer was, who the counselor was, or when this had happened. We never got to talk to her. For her to file a complaint with headquarters put everyone at a disadvantage. Had she voiced her concerns at the time we might have been able to straighten it out. It might not have been a problem at all.

The big white dog had to have been Snowball, who always took a lot of naps during play time. The rest of the dogs might have been taking a break at the time. They did get tired. The counselor might have been making notes on the dogs' paperwork.

How could we fix a problem we didn't know existed? If it had been a problem at all.

* * * *

Shy little Queenie was in the small playroom with another counselor. I was in the big room with eight rambunctious dogs, all big ones.

Without warning, the other counselor decided it was a good idea to let Queenie into the big room. This was definitely not a good idea. As soon as I saw what was happening I tried to stop it, but it was too late. The big dogs in with me spotted Queenie instantly.

As they always did with a newcomer, they mobbed around her. Poor little Queenie was sitting in a corner quivering, surrounded by a whole slew of excited dogs. She was scared silly and snapping at anyone within reach, her only means of defense. The counselor who had let her into the big room had thought Queenie might like to be in with other dogs.

I was not happy. I pushed my way through the canine welcome committee. I brushed by that counselor and the big dogs until I was able to get close enough to pick up Queenie and carry her out of harm's way. She and I went back into the smaller room and I stayed with her for the rest of the morning.

One of the things we were told in training was never to pick up a dog when other dogs are present. In this case, I had no choice. I found out why you shouldn't pick up a dog.

The other dogs jumped all over me trying to get up close to the terrified Queenie. I had to use my entire body, turn it this way and that, and do some quick side-stepping to keep them away from her. I'm sure they were just curious, but Queenie didn't know that. She was definitely not a happy camper at that moment. We did make it back to the safety of the small playroom without incident.

After that day all counselors paid attention to exactly which dog was assigned to which room. No dog was ever permanently assigned to the smaller room without good reason.

Queenie never saw the inside of the big room again. That was a good thing for all.

*　*　*　*

Yes, we occasionally had to deal with the unexpected or the unusual, but only once.

More stuff happens. You learn more.

~ Outside In ~

Large glass doors and windows separated the doggy Day Camp from the main store. We would get small audiences off and on throughout the day. Store customers would often stop just to watch the campers zooming around. Several of our camp dogs would trot over to the windows to check out these folks. Most of the dogs would give the people a glance and return to playing immediately.

Not Maggie. This Great Dane loved to check out the people. If it were allowed, she would get right up in the faces of those out in the store. Not only would she trot over to see them, she would jump up on the glass. That alone made people step back a couple of feet. Keep in mind that Maggie stood well over six feet when she was up on her hind legs. When Maggie was feeling particularly feisty, she would jump on the glass and pound it constantly with her front paws, the whole time barking for all she was worth. She had a bark more than worthy of her great size. This absolutely terrified anyone on the other side, and they generally jumped back another couple of feet. When she did this, Maggie looked pretty scary. We simply couldn't allow her to scare the daylights out of adults, kids, and the occasional puppy-in-tow. We took to escorting Maggie whenever she headed over to the windows, and we always had a lead at the ready in case she got too excited.

When she was up on the window, she was totally focused on barking and didn't want to be bothered by anyone. If anyone, canine or human, tried to distract her she would fling her head to the side and down, barking at whoever was in her space. Once I startled her by touching her shoulder.

Mostly Maggie at Doggy Day Camp

"Ouch!"

She caught my arm while she was in mid-bark. Very minor, just a mark, no broken skin, but to the people outside it must have looked like Maggie was going to rip me to shreds. I showed them my arm, gave the thumbs-up sign to let them know everything was okay. From that point on we all knew to speak to her before we touched her when she was in her ferocious mega-bark mode. It was all for show. Maggie didn't have an aggressive bone in her.

Snowball also liked to bark at people outside the windows. She had a very deep, very loud, very serious-sounding bark. She was also a pretty good sized dog, a Great Pyrenees, and tended to make people a bit nervous. They had no way of knowing what a softie Snowball really was. She didn't jump on the windows, though, and wasn't nearly as threatening as Maggie seemed to be. Snowball was just loud. Her job, as she saw it, was to bark for a minute or so at anything moving on the other side of the glass. This quickly wore her out, and she'd return to her favorite sprawl location once she was satisfied she'd properly done her job. She always did it well.

When there was someone else available to cover the playroom, I would go out and talk to our window audience. I was never a salesman, but I figured a little public relations couldn't hurt. Besides, I enjoyed talking about my campers.

Ninety percent of the time, the first question asked was, "They actually pay you to do this?"

I'd laugh and give them that old line, "Hey, it's a tough job but somebody has to do it."

Most of the adults said it looked like a great job to have. I agreed whole-heartedly. When they said they would like to have it, I told them that I wasn't ready to give mine up. Then I explained the camp program and answered questions.

I especially enjoyed it when there were little kids watching. Most of them wanted to know the names of the dogs and what kind they were. I told them the names, told them a little about each dog, and explained that the dogs were sort of in pre-school and didn't belong to us. We were just the baby-sitters. That made them laugh.

All the kids really wanted to go inside and play with the dogs. When

I told them that the dogs were not allowed to meet strangers without their own people being there, it made perfect sense to them, and they were content just to watch for a while.

Cedric, the Dachshund, was a particular favorite with children and he was a super little doggy ambassador. Because Cedric belonged to Kate, I would occasionally ask her permission to take him with me to meet the kids. I always told the kids that I had permission from his mom to bring him out of the playroom. Maggie and Snowball, because they were so big, were also favorites. They inspired awe, but the kids did not want to meet either of them face to face. Neither did most of the adults.

If a puddle appeared in the playroom, someone in the audience almost always announced, hands cupped around the mouth, "Clean-up in aisle 6." They always thought that was funny. So did I.

I was talking to some folks one day and one of them mentioned there was a ball-point pen on the floor in the middle of the playroom.

"Ah, Lady is here today," I said.

This made no sense at all to anyone but me until I explained that Lady was our resident pick-pocket, and a darned good one. I got the attention of the counselor in the playroom, pointed at the pen, and she picked it up before it became a doggy snack.

There was usually a short lull in the action at some point in the morning and in the afternoon. If onlookers happened to be watching during one of those times, they asked why the dogs weren't doing anything. I explained that dogs get tired. They didn't want to be entertained by anybody. They didn't want to play. They just wanted to rest, especially Snowball. Even wild and crazy Boomer needed to catch his breath once in a while. I suggested the people stop back by the window in ten or fifteen minutes for a livelier show.

People asked what kind of things counselors did to keep the fuzzy troops entertained. We could play ball with them, tell them stories, or lead a parade. I told them that a counselor would sometimes go to the top of the bridge and proclaim herself King of the Castle, but this usually didn't work real well. The dogs might have given a glance, but the King was ignored more often than not. So that counselor looked like a complete idiot to anyone who happened to be watching.

The people laughed and agreed that it did look pretty silly to see a counselor standing up there all alone trying to get the dogs to come on up. These people had seen me up there. They knew it looked silly. I knew it looked silly. I did it anyway.

I told them that we did not run with the dogs. Running was not a good idea at all. Oh, the dogs loved it. Most of them saw this as a great game of tag. The dogs would run up behind me and jump at my back. If it was Hotshot, the Chihuahua, jumping at the back of my calves, I was tagged and I was It.

If it happened to be Maggie jumping on my back and shoulders, however, I definitely was not It. I was knocked face down on the floor. This effectively ended the game, at least for me. The first time this happened to me was the last time. The dogs meant it all in fun, but running was definitely a thumbs-down activity.

I emphasized that we always gave them lots of affection and petting. I always told folks that we praised the dogs for every little thing. It was important. A little praise goes just as far with dogs as it does with kids and with adults, too, if you think about it.

People asked how many dogs we had in camp. Well, there were over seventy dogs that had been approved for camp. Several were in camp two or three times a week. A lot of them came occasionally. A few came in rarely. Thank goodness, they didn't all come in at the same time. We wouldn't have had room. The most we had at one time was nineteen, and I was bummed out that I had been off work that day. The fewest was two in the big room and sometimes only one in the small room. The atmosphere of the playroom on any day depended on how many and which dogs attended. I told my audience I thoroughly enjoyed the very busy days with a lot of dogs, but the occasional two-dog day was okay, too.

Our window audiences asked if the dogs were tired after a day at camp. We'd been told that when the dogs got back home they were worn out and would spend the rest of the evening just lounging about.

I let them know that worn out counselors did pretty much the same thing.

Playing with dogs is a wonderfully satisfying way to wear yourself out.

~ Good-bye, Campers ~

Being a Doggy Day Camp Counselor was the lowest paying, most physically demanding job I'd ever had. It was also the best and most rewarding job I'd ever had.

When I first decided that I wanted to work with dogs, I was quite sure it would be a job I would like. I was so right. I worked with several good people who had the same love of animals as I do. I had an opportunity to learn a great deal about dogs in general. I met an incredible number of terrific dogs, each one special in one way or another.

Even when the dogs were misbehaving it was impossible for me to get mad at them. Their antics almost always made me laugh. Even when I was dancing the Poop-Scoopin' Boogie or cleaning crates, washing dishes, and mopping the playroom floor, it just didn't seem all that much like work. It was a bonus to be getting paid for having so darned much fun.

Truth be told, I spent about ninety-nine percent of my work hours in the camp playrooms, and very little time stocking shelves, cashiering, or pricing. I did do a very little of that, but everybody knew I'd rather be in with my dogs. I didn't shirk in any area, but I did push for playroom duty. I was almost always with them. It was a good deal for the dogs. It was a fantastic deal for me. I truly loved it. So much so that I ended up staying long after I'd earned the necessary Social Security credits.

However, the time had come for me to leave.

My own good ol' dog, Toby, was getting up in years. He was having a hard time seeing and hearing. He was having an ever-harder time getting around these days. Toby needed me at home far more than the campers needed me. It wasn't easy to leave my camp dogs, but this decision hadn't required all that much thought. Toby needed me at home and there I would be. He was my first priority.

Do I miss camp? Absolutely. I must admit I don't much miss all the cleaning chores, but I sure miss all of my dogs. They made me laugh while I was with them, and they make me laugh now just thinking about them.

After I left, I stopped in to visit the camp a time or two. All my furry pals came to say a quick hello and zoomed right back to whatever the action was at the time. I was really tickled, though, the last time I visited on a Maggie day.

She spotted me through the lobby window. She started running immediately over to the kitchen Dutch door where she knew I'd end up. In her typical Maggie enthusiasm, she slipped and went to the floor, sliding on her side. She just picked herself up and kept running. We both got to the door and she put her front paws up on my shoulders, towering over me. I did not make her get down. She gave me a mega–Maggie-hug and I hugged her right back. Then she rested her big, lovable head right on the top of my head. Maggie missed me, I think, almost as much as I missed her.

Puppy-sitting with dogs who already had good homes.
I knew from the start it would work. And it did. It really did.

~ Choose Wisely ~

Some people think a day care program is completely useless. Some people think a dog day camp worker is even more useless. These people would simply be wrong.

It is a really good service for a lot of people as well as their dogs. Maggie is a case in point. Her mom lived in an apartment and worked five days a week. If Maggie did not have someplace to spend time with people who genuinely cared about her and keep her active she would have been confined to a small area for most of the day. Socializing with other dogs at the same time was an added benefit.

We had dogs whose people were elderly and couldn't exercise them much at all. It also worked out for several overweight dogs to have running room so they could shed a few pounds. A lot of our dogs came only now and then, when their families had day-long activities and if they had no place to go. These dogs would have been home alone for a very long time.

Yes, we had dogs there just because their people thought their dogs would enjoy playing with other dogs in a safe, healthy, and supervised environment. Not everyone had the time to take Fido to a dog park. Besides, there are a lot of folks, like my husband and myself, who don't want the risks of such a park. In a day camp setting, people know the dogs will all have had proper vaccinations against disease. No matter why they came to camp, all of our dogs got plenty of loving and attention while they were in our care.

It's important to remember that not every dog will do well in a day care setting. For example, older dogs don't always adjust to day camp.

Mostly Maggie at Doggy Day Camp

My own dog was a prime example of this. Toby was fourteen, well behaved, quiet, got along well with my grand-puppies at his house or theirs, and loved to have company. He was visibly relieved, though, when the visitors left his domain. He had been the only child too long and found it difficult to adapt to a large group of young and active non-family dogs. He went with me to camp only twice. He wasn't aggressive in the least, but he just didn't want to be bothered with camp dogs or activities. He was more than happy to stay home on his own bed while I went off to day camp. I left for camp before my husband went to work. Because I worked part time, Toby was home by himself, sleeping, for only about four hours during the day.

Extremely shy dogs might have a problem in a group setting. Depending on the severity of the dog's problem, a couple of suggestions are offered. Sometimes you can give the shy dog a trial period. More often than not, the wallflower will come around within a couple of days. In other instances, severe nervousness can be incredibly stressful to a dog, as was the case with Daisy. This can sometimes be overcome through proper socialization training classes, but not always. You do not want your dog sitting in a corner cowering in terror all day, and he should not be forced to endure a situation he can't handle.

Aggressive dogs, regardless of size or breed will not do well, since they are a danger to other dogs, to themselves, and to the staff. In our case, if the evaluating counselor felt that the aggression could be corrected, training classes were suggested. If the dog successfully passed such a course, he could then be re-evaluated for camp. Jeeves had gone through such a class before we met him. His people had been astonished at the difference in his behavior, and we were happy to have him in camp. Socialization classes do work in a lot of situations and should be seriously considered if your dog has problems.

If you and your furry friend are ready to look for a day care program near you, do a little research. Not all programs are the same. There is quite a variety of facilities, programs, and prices out there.

Some programs offer basic training classes and special activities as part of doggy day care. Some camps offer full professional training, socialization, and agility classes at a discounted price for campers. Some programs offer very structured activity time. Others do not. Some offer outdoor play areas and pool time. Some places even offer private rooms for your pet, complete with raised cots and televisions. On-site or adjacent vet and grooming services are available in some programs. Overnight boarding is also offered in some programs. You really do have to decide what kind of facility you want and how much you want to spend.

Each day care program will have its own criteria for accepting dogs. Some will not allow any of the so-called bully breeds such as Pit Bulls, Rottweilers, and Dobermans into a program at all. There are other places that accept these breeds, but do not allow interaction with other breeds. There are camps that fully accept these breeds. This is strictly a matter of personal feeling and comfort level for both the day care staff and the pet parents.

Not every day care uses evaluation to determine suitability for day care overall and to determine the best play group setting. Some programs immediately put new dogs in with an unfamiliar group. Personally, I prefer a program that fully considers each dog rather than just throwing my dog into an unknown situation and hoping for the best.

Not every day care insists that a dog be spayed or neutered, but they will insist on current vaccinations—at least they should. If they don't, be a little leery. You don't want to put your dog in an unhealthy environment.

Play groups might be determined by both size and temperament, large and small dogs always kept separate. While my camp played large groups of dogs, big, small, and in between, together for extended periods of time, many programs play smaller groups for several shorter periods of time throughout the day. Find the right comfort level for you and your dog.

Check out the facilities personally. Make sure all areas are properly secured. Ask for a tour. Make sure everything is clean. Cleaning and sanitizing should include toys as well as playrooms, crates, and kitchen facilities. Make sure there is an adequate system for waste disposal. While there might well be a lingering doggy odor, it should not be overwhelming.

Be sure the dogs are provided with fresh water in the playroom several times a day, and that they have water in their crates. Some places will provide lunch for a fee. Some will encourage you to pack a doggy lunch. Be sure to tell the camp staff if your dog does not eat lunch at all. Ask if the program will accommodate any special dietary needs and allergies your dog might have. Ask whether workers will administer any necessary medications you provide that your dog might need. Don't automatically assume they will do this.

Observe the playroom in action. Keep in mind that the dogs really do get tired and take a rest now and then. If this is the case on your first visit, please give it a second try at a different time of day. Ask the crew what would be a good time to see the most activity. Watch the staff with the dogs. While they might not be in the thick of the canine cavorting, they should certainly be attentive to the action. If not, ask why not.

Ask if the staff members have received any sort of training. It stands to reason that dog day care workers are dog lovers, but he or she will also need a basic understanding of dog behavior, intuitive or learned. A good staff member will have the ability to command the respect of the dogs, will have the skills to deal with unexpected situations, and will have patience for sometimes rowdy dogs. Staff members will most likely have great respect for animals in general.

The workers are there to monitor behavior and to prevent minor tiffs from becoming major scraps. Remember dogs will be dogs. Just like people, they have a bad day now and then. Keep in mind, too, that minor scratches and nips are possible, rare to be sure, but not unheard of in dog day care. Sometimes the dogs play pretty rough.

Staff members will try to anticipate behavior that is disrupting or dangerous to campers and can usually prevent aggression. It is important to remember most day care staffers are not likely to be full-fledged dog trainers. Ask what corrective action will be taken if a dog is misbehaving at an unacceptable level. Ask what systems are in place to handle any minor injury. Ask if there are evacuation procedures in place in case of emergency.

Tell the interviewer about your dog's personality. Include any little quirks he might have, his favorite toy, and activity. Be sure to tell them of any dislikes he has. For example, we were all glad we'd been told that Rambo did not like to be hugged. It most likely saved us from being bitten the first time we tried to put him into a crate. The more the day camp knows about your dog, the better off everybody will be. The more you know about the day care program, the better off everybody will be. It's a two-way street.

Ask any question that is important to you and your dog. A good day care program will encourage their workers to answer any and all of your questions and to give you helpful suggestions. Once your dog is accepted into a program, be sure to give him time to adjust. Any rough spots will quickly iron themselves out. If not, please don't subject your dog to a situation that makes him miserable. Camp should be fun for your dog, not an ordeal.

Dog people can learn the names of innumerable dogs almost instantly. It's a pretty sure bet that staff members will remember your dog's name from the moment they meet him. It's not a sure bet that the counselors will remember your name ever. Please don't take offense if they refer to you as Fido's dad or Fidette's mom. Knowing your name just doesn't seem quite as important as knowing your dog's name. All it means is that you have your dog in a program where he is instantly recognized and will get the attention he deserves. As it should be.

Remember, your dog will most likely be ready to loaf around when he gets home. That's a good sign. It means the camp counselors have kept him pretty active. Now you and your furry family member can kick back, relax, and just enjoy each other's companionship.

And isn't that what man's best friend is all about?

Author the Author
Barb Norris

I was raised in suburban Detroit with an older brother and a younger sister, and have a lot of happy childhood memories! I knew my husband, Tom, from both high school and church, and we were married in 1970. We are blessed with two wonderful daughters, two terrific sons-in-law, and two fantastic grandkids. Our family also includes rescued pets; Molly, a dog of unknown ancestry, Bailey the cat, and two grand-puppies; a Greyhound rescue named Gunner, and a Golden Retriever mix named Baxter.

Most of my married life I was a happy-to-stay-at-home mom. I did work off and on in various office positions, and was a freelance artist. I've sold several pet portraits and wild duck paintings. Because my hands have become a bit unsteady over the years, I rarely paint these days. Instead, I write. My first book, *Mostly Maggie at Doggy Day Camp* is based on my experiences in the lowest-paying, most fun and most rewarding job I've ever had. I was a doggy day camp counselor, the perfect job for me. I absolutely loved it!

I'm now retired and plan to spend more time writing. And when I grow up I'm going to raise horses.